D1478227

Chase

Chase

An American Extreme Bull Riders Tour Romance

Barbara Dunlop

WITHDRAWN FROM
RAPIDES PARISH LIBRARY

TULE
PUBLISHING

RAPIDES PARISH LIBRARY
Alexandria, Louisiana

Chase

Copyright © 2017 Barbara Dunlop
Tule Publishing First Printing, May 2017
The Tule Publishing Group, LLC

ALL RIGHTS RESERVED

No part of this book may be used or reproduced in any manner
whatsoever without written permission except in the case of brief
quotations embodied in critical articles and reviews.

This is a work of fiction. Names, characters, places, and incidents are
products of the author's imagination or are used fictitiously. Any
resemblance to actual events, locales, organizations, or persons, living or
dead, is entirely coincidental.

ISBN: 978-1-946772-66-4

Prologue

CHASE GARRETT STARED at his best friend's pickup truck parked in front of Chase's fiancée's yellow clapboard bungalow in the wheatgrass covered foothills of the Rocky Mountains. Patrick's black V-8 dually wouldn't have been an unusual sight—he and Laura-Leigh had known each other since the third grade. But it was four a.m. and the house was full dark.

Chase supposed Patrick might have tied one on last night and decided against driving home. Not that the dirt roads of the Twin River Valley were diligently patrolled for tipsy cowboys. But it was a possibility.

Thing was, Chase had been away the past two weeks. He was home early and all set to surprise Laura-Leigh with news she'd been waiting for, a decision that would make her very happy.

He stepped from his pickup, firmly shutting the door, adamantly refusing to keep the noise level low. Sneaking up to the house would mean allowing for the unacceptable. It would mean he was suspicious. He wasn't. There was a perfectly acceptable explanation for Patrick's presence.

He thumped his boot heels on the wooden porch. If anything, he was louder than usual.

"Laura-Leigh?" he called out as he opened the front door. "Honey? I'm back."

There was a thud and a shuffle beyond her bedroom door.

The sofa was empty and the door to the small guest room stood open.

Chase flipped on the overhead light. Its beam showed him a neatly made bed in the guest room, its champagne-colored bedspread wrinkle free, pillows untouched, the green plaid, wool blanket folded in its usual spot at the foot of the bed.

Frantic whispers sounded behind the bedroom door. Two voices, one a woman's and one a man's.

He thought about leaving. Then he thought about doubling up his fists. In the end, he folded his arms across his chest and waited, letting the outrage pulse its way through his brain as he struggled to come to terms with the appalling reality.

The bedroom door opened a crack.

"Chase?" Laura-Leigh's whisper was paper dry.

She appeared in her white thigh-length nightgown. It was worn flannel, the lace on the scooped neck frayed in two places. It wasn't what a woman wore for her first time with a man. This had happened before.

Her cheeks were flushed and her brown eyes were wide

with obvious fear. And she drew the door tightly closed behind her. As if Chase would be too stupid to notice she had a man in her bed.

"You're early," she said, her back pressed flat against the door.

"His pickup's in the driveway," Chase said.

The color drained from her face.

The door opened behind her and she staggered back a small step.

Patrick wasn't going to leave her to face Chase alone. Normally, Chase would give the man points for that. But there was nothing normal about this. Laura-Leigh was pregnant with Chase's baby, and their wedding date was less than a month away.

"I should take your head off," he growled at Patrick.

"You can try," Patrick responded.

Chase clamped his fists by his side and took a step forward. His best friend might have had his back in barroom brawls from Calgary to Denver, but Chase was going to pulverize him all the same.

"Chase, no!" Laura-Leigh cried.

"You're defending *him*?" Chase asked her in astonishment.

"I can handle him," Patrick told her.

Chase had expected an abject apology from Laura-Leigh. He'd expected her to throw herself into his arms and beg his forgiveness for her indiscretion. He wouldn't have forgiven her. What man could do that? But he had expected her to try.

"It's not Patrick's fault," she cried. "It just sort of—"

"Don't you dare tell me it just *happened*. Betraying your fiancé doesn't *just happen*."

"Chase, man." Patrick stepped out from behind Laura-Leigh, one hand outstretched.

"You want to go at it?" Chase asked.

He was ready for a fight. He was more than ready. He felt like he was seeing his best friend clearly for the first time. And he hated what he saw.

"We didn't mean for you to find out this way," Patrick said.

"You didn't mean for me to find out *at all*." Of that, Chase was sure. "What kind of degenerate are you? We're engaged. She's pregnant with my child."

Patrick and Laura-Leigh exchanged a guilty look.

Reality slammed into Chase's skull with the force of a cinderblock.

"No!" he roared, and he lunged at Patrick.

Patrick took the first punch without defending himself.

But then he struck back. Whether it was reflex, or whether he realized that Chase was actually going to kill him, Chase couldn't be sure. But he tasted blood from a cut lip, and he threw another punch, this one connecting with Patrick's solar plexus.

Patrick hunched over, but had it in him to return an uppercut, which sent Chase sprawling.

"Stop!" Laura-Leigh screamed. "Stop it, both of you!"

Patrick hesitated, while Chase regrouped. He wasn't stopping, no way, no how. Patrick deserved everything Chase was set to dish out.

But Laura-Leigh stepped in front of Patrick again, and Chase instantly pulled himself up short.

"You're going to hide behind her?" he shouted at Patrick.

"This is getting us nowhere," Patrick said.

"You son-of-a-bitch."

"We tried to fight it," Patrick said. "We tried like hell to fight it, man."

"Obviously," Chase drawled, his mouth curling into a sneer. "You tried so hard, you got her pregnant."

He could feel his world slipping away. He'd just sold his spread in Lethbridge. He was coming back to his hometown full time to raise his child on his family's land. It was what Laura-Leigh wanted, and it was what he thought she deserved.

"I thought the baby was yours," Laura-Leigh said to Chase.

"Do you have any idea how awful that sounds?" Chase asked.

"I did a test," she said. "Last week. And..." Her voice trailed away.

"It could have been either of ours?" Chase glared at Patrick. "What's the matter with you? What *is* the matter with you?"

"I didn't know what to do," Patrick said, looking guilty but defiant at the same time.

Chase leaned forward. "Let me give you a tip for the future. When in doubt, you don't *screw* your best friend's fiancée."

Since it was either go through Laura-Leigh to get to Patrick or leave, Chase turned on his heel.

He marched out of the house, slammed his way into his pickup, rammed the gas pedal, and snaked down the driveway in a hail of dust and flying stones.

He made one stop on his way out of town, at the little house where he'd grown up and lived part-time for the past five years. There was only one thing he wanted there, only one thing he needed—an unopened letter from the AEBR, the American Extreme Bull Riders Tour.

He didn't have to open it to know what it was. It was an invitation to join the bull-riding circuit. And on the circuit was exactly where he was going. His spread in Lethbridge belonged to someone else now. And the Twin River Valley would never be his home again.

Chase was leaving, and he wasn't coming back.

Chapter One

THE LAST PLACE on earth Madeline Barrett wanted to be on a Saturday night in Deadwood, South Dakota was the American Extreme Bull Riders Tour event. But her three-year-old son, Riley, had worn her down.

Along with his tiny blue jeans, scuffed red cowboy boots, and a pressed white cotton shirt, he had a mini Stetson perched on his head. He swung his legs where they dangled from the battered wooden benches of the friends and family stand, leaning eagerly forward, eyes fixed on the ring.

Anticipation was rife through the crowd as the hot summer sun touched the Black Hills to the east. Music blared from the speakers during a break from the announcer's patter, and the riders were prepping behind the chutes filled with muscular bulls.

The sights, smells, and sounds were all familiar to Maddy. They were also bittersweet. Her husband Chase had been happiest here. Even knowing how it had ended for him, far too soon last September, he would have stepped into the chute, rosined his rope, wrapped his hand, and let the world go insane beneath him. It was what he claimed he needed to feel alive.

"Is Daddy here tonight?" Riley asked.

The unexpected question, so innocently delivered, blind-sided Maddy. For a moment she couldn't answer.

"Sweetheart." She took Riley's hand and bent her head close to his so she could speak softly. "You know Daddy's in heaven."

Riley looked up at her, nodding. "Uncle Zane said there are bulls to ride in heaven."

Her heart squeezed tight and she gave Riley a kiss on the top of his head. "I'm sure there are, sweetheart."

"Daddy said he'd come home after the ride." Riley looked straight ahead now, squinting at the activity around the chutes.

Maddy was at a loss. She'd explained to Riley that Chase wasn't coming home this time; that he was in heaven now. It had never occurred to her that Riley saw heaven as just another bull-riding town.

"There's Uncle Zane." She pointed in an attempt to distract him. "See his red shirt?"

"He's riding Cyclone tonight," Riley said with an air of knowledge that belied his age. "Cyclone has wicked spins."

"Did Uncle Zane tell you that?"

Riley shot her a look of impatience. "No. I watched it for myself on TV. Can I get mini-doughnuts, Mommy?"

For the moment, Maddy was relieved to let the conversation move on. "Sure. At the break before the finals, okay?"

The announcer called the first bull ride, directing the crowd's attention to chute three and introducing the rider and the bull.

The pair burst out of the chute, the bull rocking straight into the air, then into an immediate buck. Riley came to his feet, while Maddy held her breath.

The rider's form looked good. He was centered, and his arm was high, legs working. But then the bull twisted right, unsettling him. It twisted left. When the rider came down, there was nothing but air beneath his butt. He went straight to the ground, kicking his leg free of the bull's back.

Maddy cringed, as he thudded to the dirt.

The three brightly dressed bullfighters moved in to distract the bull and protect the rider. The rider leapt to his feet and sprinted for the fence, while the bull trotted the length of the ring, tossing its head, looking for something to charge. The safety rider on horseback, ambled after it, readying his lasso to lead the bull away.

"Tough luck, cowboy," Riley said, sitting back down on the bench.

Maddy couldn't help but smile as her son parroted her brother Zane. Three of her four brothers still frequented the Deadwood area, and she was grateful for the time they'd spent with Riley since Chase's death.

The announcer called the next rider.

He stayed on, but barely, scoring a seventy-one. The next three were bucked off, followed by an impressive ride of eighty-five point five by a Texas cowboy. The crowds gave a rousing cheer and the rider waved his hat in acknowledgement.

"Ladies and gentlemen, our next rider has an impressive record, including recent wins in Santa Fe and Reno."

Chute one was pulled open and a pure black bull burst out. The cowboy was tall, settled square on the bull and seeming to stick like glue. His hand was high in the air, his form near perfect.

As the crowd cheered loudly, the announcer's voice grew excited. "Chase Garrett is riding Hammerfall, and showing us all how it's done."

"Mommy!" Riley grabbed onto Maddy's arm, shaking it. "It's *Daddy*. He's here!"

Maddy's stomach bottomed out. "No, sweetheart."

Riley climbed up on the bench to stand as tall as possible. "Go, Daddy, go!" he called out. "Ride 'im!"

"Honey, honey." Maddy wrapped an arm around Riley's waist, steadying him. "That's not Daddy. That's a different cowboy."

"He said his name." Riley's eyes were alight with excitement.

"There are lots of cowboys named Chase."

The horn sounded and the rider dismounted, tossing his hat in the air. His grin was wide and Maddy herself did a double take. There was no denying the resemblance to her late husband.

"Daddy!" Riley shouted.

Before she could stop him, Riley was down off the bench and running along the stands.

"Riley, no!"

But he was beyond listening.

She jumped to her feet, grabbing her tote bag and rushing after him. She called for him to stop, but there was too much noise. The crowd was cheering, and the announcer was shouting congratulations to the rider.

"How about a ninety-two?" the announcer called out. "The high score of the night so far. Let's show Chase just what we think of that effort."

The crowd cheered louder while the bullfighters tried to coral the black bull.

Riley ran along the platform, past the crowded stands toward the chutes and the cowboys.

"Riley," she called louder as he ducked and weaved through the spectators.

She was gaining and she was easily keeping him in sight. But she was worried about what she'd say when she caught him. They needed to leave the event. They needed to go home and have a long talk about death and what that meant.

He'd barely turned three when Chase had died. It was so much for a young boy to comprehend. He was coming up on his fourth birthday now, and she thought he'd been able to wrap his head around it. He talked about his daddy being in heaven. Until tonight, she hadn't realized heaven to Riley was still the same as Cheyenne, Omaha or Billings.

Then he stopped.

Thank goodness.

"Riley, honey," she called out.

"Daddy." He reached his hand through the rails of the fence. He was on the stand's walkway, four feet off the ground, and the rider named Chase was coming in his direction.

"Daddy," he repeated, his little hand grasping the air.

When the man walked right past him, Maddy thought her heart would break into two.

Riley shrieked his disappointment. Then he ducked his head and called out again. In a split-second, he was through the rails and falling onto the dirt of the ring.

The spectators in the vicinity gasped. Then they began to shout. The bull swung his head toward the commotion.

Crying and wiping dust from his eyes, Riley stood up.

Maddy ran for the rail, her heart thumping in abject terror.

The bull lowered its head and ran for Riley.

The bullfighters shouted, running and jumping, trying desperately to draw the bull's attention away from Riley.

The man named Chase turned. He saw what was happening and dropped his rigging, sprinting for Riley. He and the bull were in a dead heat.

Maddy grabbed the top rail, intending to vault over, but someone grabbed her.

"You'll never get there," they shouted in her ear. "You'll only make it worse."

She struggled to break the hold. "Let me go! That's my son."

The bull was closing in. Riley was crying and rubbing his eye, he was about to be trampled or gored.

She screamed and Chase launched himself between the bull and Riley, grabbing her son in his arms and rolling beneath the feet of the charging bull. The bull's front foot caught him square in the back, but he remained protectively curled around Riley.

Then the bullfighters arrived, shouting and circling. One of them smacked the bull in the head. Another hit it on the rump. The third had peeled off his bright-colored shirt and waved it like a flag.

It worked.

They distracted the bull. Chase scrambled up the fence, launching over the top with Riley in his arms, pulling them both out of harm's way.

ADRENALIN PUMPED THROUGH Chase as his feet hit the solid flooring of the grandstands. A pain shot through his side, but he kept his death grip on the young boy who'd fallen into the ring.

"Thank you. Thank you so much." A woman's breathless

voice penetrated above the announcer and the cheers of the crowd. People pressed in around them, obviously concerned about the young boy and hoping to learn he was alright.

"Daddy." The young boy sobbed, his little arms wrapped tightly around Chase's neck.

He sounded upset but strong.

Chase was fairly confident the boy hadn't been hurt, but he'd feel better once the medics had a chance to look at him.

"Riley," the woman said, putting her hand on the boy's trembling back, "Mommy's here, honey."

Chase looked down to see a pretty, dark-haired woman, her blue eyes bright with unshed tears. Her face was pale and her deep red mouth was tight with concern. She had a spray of freckles across her cheekbones. It was an irrelevant fact that somehow registered in his brain.

She was fresh-faced, no makeup, but she had dark lashes that framed the most beautiful eyes he'd ever seen. Her thick hair was pulled up in a ponytail. She wore a moss green T-shirt with capped sleeves over a pair of faded jeans. She was local. He'd bet she was local.

She tried to gather her son from Chase's arms and Chase tried to hand the boy over, knowing he needed his mother's comfort.

But the boy wouldn't let go. He gripped tighter to Chase's neck.

"Daddy," he moaned tearfully.

Chase lifted his brows to the woman in a silent question.

"He's confused," she said. "He saw you ride."

The explanation didn't make any sense to Chase. He knew the boy had dirt in his eyes. Maybe he simply couldn't see.

"Your mother's here," he told the boy.

"No, Daddy, no!"

"Riley." The woman's voice was sharper than Chase thought necessary.

"Daddy, don't go," Riley wailed.

Two medics appeared, a man and a woman, both of them zeroing in on Riley.

"We need to check him out," the man told Chase.

"Please do." Chase had no intention of stopping them.

A security guard also arrived and began moving the crowd away to give the medics space.

The female medic moved behind Chase.

"His eyes are full of dirt," she announced.

"We'll need to move you to the tent," the man said. "I'm Jason," he told Chase. Then he looked to the woman. "This is your son?"

"I'm Maddy Barrett," she said. "His name is Riley."

"Riley," the medic said, "does anything hurt?"

Riley didn't answer; he simply clung tighter to Chase.

Chase looked at Maddy. "We should move this to the medical tent."

Whatever was upsetting the boy, Chase couldn't imagine it was being helped by all of the commotion. The announcer had moved on to the next bull ride, and the crowd was gradually settling back in their seats, but there was still interest in him and in Riley.

The woman named Maddy gave a rapid nod. "Yes, thank you."

Chase started to walk.

"Anything hurt on you?" the female medic asked Chase.

"I'm good," Chase said.

"The bull stepped on you."

"Took a kick to my side," Chase acknowledged as they made their way down the stairs to the area beside the stalls.

"You'll need an x-ray."

"I'm hurt, not injured." Chase could still breathe, and the pain was dull more than it was sharp. His ribs weren't broken. They were only bruised. He'd felt the same pain many times before.

His score would no doubt put him in the finals, up in just over an hour. He needed to walk it off not lay around under an x-ray machine.

They entered the relative calm of the medical tent. It was built over a rubberized plywood floor, with bright lighting, three stretchers, and basic medical equipment.

Chase carried Riley to the closest stretcher.

"The man has to put you down now, honey," Maddy said to Riley.

"No." Riley moaned, his face pressed against Chase's chest. "Please don't go, Daddy."

There was something about the boy's vulnerability that got to Chase. A protective instinct welled up inside him. He knew it was only temporary. In minutes, maybe only seconds, Riley was going to realize his mistake.

But that led Chase to a question. Who was Riley's father? Where was he? Chase was new enough to the AEBR circuit that he didn't know everyone. But if Riley's father was another rider, shouldn't he be here taking care of his son?

Maddy put her hand on Riley's shoulder, working her fingers against Chase's chest. "Riley, you need to let go."

Riley shook his head.

Maddy looked at Chase, an abject apology on her face. "He's confused," she said again.

The female medic, obviously deciding to go with the flow, put a stethoscope to Riley's back.

"Can you breathe in for me?" she asked Riley. "Nice and deep."

The boy took a deep breath while she listened.

"Can you show me your eyes?" she asked him. "Just turn your head toward me and blink. Your daddy doesn't have to put you down."

Again, Riley did as he was asked.

"I'm so sorry," Maddy whispered to Chase.

"Maybe you can call his father?" Chase suggested, growing impatient.

If Riley's father was here on the grounds, he might want to get his ass over here and help his wife and his traumatized son.

Maddy swallowed instead of answering. The abject sadness in her eyes gave Chase the answer. He could have kicked himself for his insensitivity.

"He was a bull rider?" Chase guessed.

Maddy nodded. "You look a lot like him."

Chase's arms involuntarily contracted around Riley. "How long?" he asked Maddy.

"Nine months. Last September in Nashville."

Now that he had a date, Chase knew of the incident.

The medic moved around Chase to speak to Maddy. "We're going to need to rinse his eyes."

"Okay," Maddy agreed.

"Can you hold him?" the medic asked Chase.

"I'm not—" Chase stopped himself. He had no intention of allowing Riley to continue in his delusion, but perhaps this very second wasn't the time to make things clear. "Sure," he said instead.

"Hey, buckaroo," he said to Riley. "I'm going to sit us down. You can stay in my lap if you want. But the medic is going to have to get your face and your eyes really wet. Your eyes must hurt right now."

Riley nodded.

"I've had dirt in mine too and had them rinsed out. The water will feel funny, but it doesn't hurt very much. And you'll feel better after. That be okay?"

"Yes, sir," Riley said.

"You're very brave," Chase said.

Maddy put a trembling hand to her mouth.

"I'm not finding any other injuries," the medic said to Maddy.

"Thank you." Maddy's voice was hoarse with emotion.

"We have to get to you next," the male medic told Chase in a no-nonsense voice.

"I'm fine," Chase reiterated. "Just take care of the boy."

He sat down on the stretcher, positioning Riley in his lap. The medic wheeled up a tray with an eyewash bottle and some towels.

"It would help to get your flak jacket off," the male medic said.

Chase frowned at him. "You're not going to give it a rest are you?"

"Do you want to make your next ride?"

Chase grimaced. "Fine. Go for it."

He peeled up the Velcro and pulled his left arm out of the vest. Then he popped the snaps on his black shirt. The medic anchored the sleeve while Chase shrugged his way clear.

The man's thumbs pressed on the sore spot and Chase sucked in a breath.

"You will need an x-ray," the medic said.

"Sure. After my ride." Chase would be happy to pop down to the local hospital at the end of the evening. He had no other plans.

Riley squirmed in his lap as the female medic sloshed the water through his eyes.

"Keep them open," she told him.

Riley tried, blinking rapidly against the unfamiliar sensation. But he didn't cry and he didn't complain. Chase couldn't help but be impressed.

"I can tape your ribs," the medic offered.

"Thanks," Chase said.

He'd take the extra support. The prime Harper Bucking Bulls were saved for the finals, and there was no doubt he'd have a jarring ride.

Zane Merrick appeared, striding through the tent entrance, zeroing in on the little group.

"Maddy," he said, "I didn't realize it was Riley. Is he hurt?"

"He's fine," Maddy answered.

"Nice pickup, Chase," Zane said with obvious gratitude.

Chase gave a nod of acknowledgement, waiting for someone to elaborate on Zane's interest. The two had met on several occasions over the past few months. But Zane had a tight group of friends and Chase was the new guy. They didn't exactly hang out between events.

"Zane is my brother," Maddy said.

"We're all done here," the female medic said, setting down the wash bottle and patting Riley's face dry. She looked to Maddy. "From what I can see, he's going to be just fine. You may want to follow up with your family doctor on

Monday."

"We will," Maddy said.

At the same time, Zane crouched down next to Riley. "Hey, little buddy."

Riley drew back against Chase's chest.

Zane shot Chase a look of confusion.

In turn, Chase looked up at Maddy, lobbing it to her for an explanation. He couldn't honestly figure any of this out. Riley's eyes were clear now. He could see again. He'd been listening to Chase speak for coming up on twenty minutes, and he wasn't backing away from his assertion that Chase was his father.

THOUGH THE IMMEDIATE danger was over, Maddy was grateful to now have her twin brother Zane at her side.

"How was your ride?" she automatically asked him.

"It should get me there." Then he waved away the question as unimportant, taking Maddy's arm and drawing her out of Riley's earshot. "What happened here? How did he fall into the ring? And Riley knows Chase Garrett? Do *you* know Chase Garrett?"

"Riley heard Chase's name on the loudspeaker, and he bolted from the stands."

Zane shrugged in incomprehension.

"Chase Garrett sounds an awful lot like Chase Barrett."

Zane's jaw dropped. "No way."

Maddy tried her best to give a concise explanation. "Riley said you told him there were bulls to ride in heaven."

"Sure," Zane said. "Why wouldn't there be?"

"I don't think he understands the difference between heaven and Baton Rouge or Tulsa. In his mind, each of those are places were his daddy goes to ride bulls and then comes home again."

Zane's gaze shifted to Riley and Chase. "He thinks his daddy is coming back?"

"He thinks his daddy *has* come back. This Chase looks a lot like our Chase." Maddy wouldn't exactly call it uncanny, but the resemblance was there in the jaw and around his gray eyes, and strangely, in his expression when he frowned.

"He's way taller," Zane said.

"He's a lot bigger," Maddy agreed. "But relative to Riley, they're both big."

"Riley can't seriously believe…"

"It can't last," Maddy agreed. "But I think he wants so badly to believe"—her voice caught—"that his daddy is home."

Zane drew her into his arms. "Oh, Maddy. You don't need this on top of everything else."

She leaned into her brother, drawing strength for as long as she dared. Then she squared her shoulders. She forced herself to draw back.

"I'll have to cope."

"You always cope."

"My son needs me."

"Yes, he does." Zane's gaze strayed to Chase again. "Did he just play along?"

"I don't think he knew how to react. He was pretty great about it."

"He joined the tour after Cooper broke his leg. So far, he seems like a decent guy."

Maddy also looked over at Chase Garrett. The medic was taping his ribs. It had to hurt, and holding Riley in his lap couldn't be helping. But his expression was stoic.

His gaze met hers and a surge of gratitude and admiration washed over her. At huge risk to himself, he had saved her son's life.

"I have to…" She didn't know what she was going to say or do, but she had to try to express her gratitude.

She left Zane behind and walked back to Chase.

He was attempting to put his arm back into the sleeve of his shirt.

"How can I possibly thank you?" she asked simply.

He gave her a smile. It turned to a grimace as he struggled with the sleeve.

She reached out to help, holding the sleeve opening in place so he could slip his hand in. Then she pulled it up to his shoulder, her fingers grazing his bare, hot skin. Some kind of energy seemed to emanate from him. She put it down to raw strength.

It felt good. And it made her feel strangely safe. She gave into temptation and took a step further into his aura, drawing the sides of his shirt together, clicking the snaps one by one.

He looked up, but she didn't dare meet his gaze. It was gratitude she was feeling, but it was also attraction, and that attraction was layered with a completely inappropriate arousal. Chase Garret was sexy. He was rugged and protective, and about as sexy a man as she had ever met.

"No need to thank me, ma'am." His voice was gravely deep.

Her husband had had a deep voice. It was yet another piece of Riley's fantasy that would fit. She found herself noting his earthy scent: grass, fresh air and horses. It was cowboy through and through.

"You saved his life," she said.

She'd finished with the snaps, but she didn't step back.

Instead, she gave in and looked into his eyes.

"I'd have done it for anyone. A child, a cowboy... you."

Her chest contracted, and she drew in a jerky breath.

"I'm just glad I was there," he said.

"You made sure you got there." Her mind flashed back to the critical seconds, Chase's lightning fast sprint, his dive in front of the rampaging bull, the way he rolled his body around Riley. If he hadn't done everything so fast, so right...

"Don't do that," he said to her. "I can see where your mind's going. Don't let it. I got to him. That's all that matters."

"You could have—"

He covered her hand with his. "I didn't. I made it. Your son is safe."

"Daddy?"

Chase's eyes clouded for the briefest of seconds.

"Riley, honey," she said, crouching down to draw him into her arms, "you have to come with Mommy now."

"No."

Chase rustled Riley's hair. "I have to go ride now, buckaroo."

Riley looked at Chase. "You're going to ride another bull?"

"I made the finals. So, yes, I'm going to ride another bull."

Riley sat more fully upright. "Eight seconds?"

Chase gave an eye-crinkling smile. "Eight seconds."

Riley lifted his hand for a high five, and Chase gave him a light smack on the palm.

Maddy's chest nearly caved with emotion. For an instant, her husband was back, and Riley had a father once again.

Riley sobered, looking up at Chase. "You'll come back after?"

It was obvious Chase didn't know how to answer the question.

Zane's hearty voice broke in. "Sure, we'll be back. We're not going anywhere. We both made the final ten."

Maddy shot her brother a look of surprise. It might be tough, but it was better to end this thing now. Riley would be upset, but he was going to be just as upset later when they had to say goodbye to Chase.

Zane reached out to brush the tip of Maddy's nose. "This'll wait, Matilda. We've got us some bulls to ride."

Riley finally slid off Chase's lap and took Maddy's hand.

Chase came carefully to his feet. "Matilda?" he asked her in an undertone.

"I hate it. He uses it when he thinks I'm being too fussy."

"You're not too fussy."

"Thank you."

"And you're not too blasé." He started to walk. "You, Madeline, are just right."

Riley took a hop and a skip between them. "What bull are you ridin', Daddy?"

"How did you know Madeline was my real name?" she asked Chase.

"Lucky guess."

"You're ridin' Lucky Guess?" Riley took Chase's hand as well.

"They haven't done the draw yet. But all the Harper Bucking Bulls are tough."

"Are they ornery?" Riley asked. "Stubborn as mules? Do they jump sky high?"

"All of the above," Chase said with an indulgent smile.

"Then you should get a gooood ride."

"I expect I will."

"Will you win another buckle?"

"Riley," Maddy said. "You need to let Chase focus."

She swung her son up into her arms. There was something too intimate about him walking between the two of them.

They came to the junction of the stands and the stalls. It was time to say goodbye to Chase. One of the cowboys tossed Chase his lost hat, and he caught it in midair to plunk it on his head. She detected the slightest of grimaces as he moved.

"Hurt?" she asked.

"It's nothing."

"Thank you, Chase," she said one more time.

He tipped his hat and smiled. "Happy to be of service, ma'am."

And then he was gone. And Riley was smiling. And Maddy's heart felt ever so slightly lighter.

It was a rebound reaction, she assured herself. After such intense fear and danger, she should expect to feel better than usual. And she did.

Chapter Two

C HASE HAD HAD some odd experiences in his twenty-seven years, but nothing came close to the past hour with Riley Barrett and his mother Madeline. He'd never met Chase Barrett, and nobody had ever mentioned a resemblance. But obviously there was something there beyond the similar name. Riley wasn't playacting. He was convinced Chase was his father.

His heart went out to Madeline. He'd guess she had a tough haul ahead of her, explaining to her son that his daddy hadn't come back.

Perched on the fence behind chute number five, activity all around him, rock music blaring from the speakers, dust whirling up in the evening breeze, he waited his turn in the finals. The first two cowboys had been bucked off. Then Rory Douglas scored an eight-six. It was a solid score. Combined with his points yesterday and his earlier ride today, he was comfortably in the number one spot.

Chase scanned the crowd, easily spotting Madeline sitting next to her son in row three. The floodlights reflected off her face, her expression attentive as she waited for the current competitor to leave the chute. It was clear she appreciated the sport, which made sense if she'd been married to a rider.

He tried to guess her age, early twenties, maybe. She must have been awfully young when she had Riley. He couldn't help wonder at the story behind that. He assumed there was a story. And then he wondered what it was about her that had his curiosity going.

"Chase?" Zane Merrick interrupted Chase's thoughts, stepping up on the third rail to come level with him.

"Hey," Chase greeted, though he kept his gaze on Madeline.

With the top combined score over Friday and Saturday's rides, Zane was riding tenth in the final round, right after Chase.

"Wanted to say thanks again." Zane held out his hand.

Chase reluctantly took his gaze off Madeline. He peeled off his glove to shake. "Not a problem."

"I'm not just talking about the rescue."

"Sure. Still, not a problem." Chase was confident any man on the circuit would have done exactly the same as him.

"I don't know what got into Riley."

"I take it I look something like his father." It was the only reasonable conclusion.

Zane gave a shrug. "I wouldn't have noticed on my own."

Chase coughed out a short chuckle. "Glad to hear it. I

haven't been paying much attention to your looks either."

Zane grinned. "But now that Maddy's pointed it out."

"She sees it?" Chase's gaze immediately returned to Madeline in the stands.

He couldn't help but wonder what that meant. Did it make her sad? Did it bring back the pain of her loss? He hoped not. He sure wouldn't want to cause her any additional grief.

"It's there," Zane said. "He's only three, and his dad's been gone for nearly a year."

Since Chase was human, his heart went out to the kid. "I wish I knew how to help."

"You didn't blow him off."

Chase couldn't help but be offended at the very suggestion. "What guy's going to blow him off?"

Riley seemed like a wonderful kid. What grown man would knowingly hurt him?

"Some might. Some might not. Anyway, I wanted to say thanks for being patient with him."

"He'll figure it out." Chase was sure of that.

But for an odd moment, he hoped it took a while. He'd take another hug from the kid. He'd sure take a handshake a hug or anything else from his mom. When she'd brushed his bare shoulder earlier, he felt like he'd been branded.

He hadn't been with a woman since Laura-Leigh six months ago, so he supposed that might explain the intense reaction. He was still recovering from the breakup, and he wasn't about to get involved in any kind of relationship. And none of the buckle bunnies tempted him in the least.

But he was tempted by Madeline. He was very tempted. He decided to take it as a good sign.

"What?" Zane asked, bringing him back to reality.

Chase corralled his thoughts. "What, what?"

"You've got a funny look on your face."

"I'm thinking about my ride."

Zane rapped his hand on the top of the fence. "Looks like you're planning to enjoy your ride a whole lot more than I'm planning to enjoy mine."

Chase looked down at Road to Ruin, nicknamed Rocky. The veteran bull was twitching in the chute, tossing his head and pawing the ground. Chase shifted and felt the sharp bite of his ribs. Enjoy was definitely too strong a word.

He touched his hand to his sore ribs. Now that his adrenalin had worn off, he realized the injury was worse than he'd thought. He was still going to ride, but he'd better darn well stay on the bull all the way to the horn. Because landing anywhere but on his feet was going to hurt like hell.

"You ready, Chase?" one of the stock hands asked.

"You bet." Chase stuffed his hand back into his glove and stepped across the narrow chute, positioning himself above the bull's back.

Zane clapped him on the shoulder. "See you on the other side."

"Good luck, man," Chase responded.

Zane gave him a cocky grin and then dropped to the ground.

Chase turned all of his attention to Rocky. He put a foot on the bull's back to let the animal know he was there. His rope man, Buddy Roberts, held Chase's rope taut while Chase rubbed the rosin to warm it. Then he settled his butt on the bull and put his hand through the handle to wrap his rope.

"He favors left on the way out," the handler said, "and his head goes way low."

The bull reared up, and someone grabbed Chase's flak jacket to make sure he didn't fall. His feet were solid on the fence rails. He wasn't about to go anywhere. The bull quickly settled.

"Ready?" the gate man called.

Chase stuck his left arm in the air and gave a nod.

The gate opened wide and Rocky flew out. Sure enough, he turned left, and his head went low. Chase stuck to his back, anchoring his hand and holding on with all the strength in his arm. His shoulder burned with the effort.

Rocky's back legs went high, and Chase leaned backward, holding out his free arm to keep his form. His injured ribs jarred, and he grunted in pain. He was two seconds in. He was hurting, but things were holding together. He kicked with his legs. He didn't wear spurs, but the form was the same.

Rocky went straight up in the air. Straight was good. He

could handle straight and high. But then thebull spun right. And when Chase expected it to correct, it kept going, three hundred and sixty degrees, and then another three-sixty. Its head went low, and its back legs high.

Chase battled to keep form. He knew the horn was less than a second away.

It sounded, and the crowd roared.

As he released his rope, his gaze went involuntarily to Madeline. She was on her feet. Riley was standing on the bench, they were both cheering madly. It was the first time since joining the AEBR tour that he'd had individual spectators. It felt good.

Then Rocky suddenly twisted and kicked, jolting Chase, breaking his grip and sending him sprawling.

He had a fleeting image of Madeline's horrified expression as he flew through the air. Then he landed on his back, and he felt an agonizing jolt to his injured ribs. Rocky's face and horns filled his vision. But the bullfighters were there in an instant, drawing the animal away. Rocky knew the drill and headed for the exit.

Chase rolled to his feet. He waved his hat to the crowd to show he was okay. His vision was blurred, and his ribs were on fire. He forced himself to put one foot in front of the other as he marched to the exit gate.

The medics were there to meet him.

"The ribs?" the male medic asked.

Chase swore.

"I'll bet," the man said, helping him to the medical tent while the crowd behind them cheered for Zane. "Breathing alright?"

"Yes," Chase managed.

The intense pain was moving to a throb. That was a good sign.

"You didn't puncture a lung," the medic said.

"I didn't puncture anything." Chase grimaced as he sat down. "But they might be cracked this time."

"They were cracked last time," said the medic.

A few minutes later, Buddy Roberts appeared in the tent doorway. "You're number one, Chase."

Chase gave him a thumb's up.

"Zane got a ninety even. One seventy-seven overall. You ended with one seventy-nine five."

Chase started to stand.

"Whoa," the medic said. "You're not going anywhere."

"I'll get an x-ray in the morning," Chase said. "Right now, I'm picking up my belt and my check."

Buddy moved to help him.

"I got it," Chase said, waving away the offer. He didn't need a nurse, at least not one that looked like Buddy.

"You sure?" Buddy asked.

"You guys are lunatics," the medic said.

"Gotta pay the bills," Chase said. He was still killer sore, but the payday would help ease the pain. So would a couple of shots of whiskey at the afterparty.

He made his way back to the ring where the announcer was killing time, waiting for him to appear for photos. He quickly announced Chase's presence, and Chase pasted a smile on his face, meeting up with the sponsor at the end of the ring, accepting the weekend's belt buckle and his check.

On his way out, Zane was there to congratulate him. Chase returned the congratulations, since Zane was well into the money and staying in the top five on points as well.

"Daddy, Daddy!" called Riley's voice.

The boy came rocketing through the crowd, obviously intent on throwing himself into Chase's arms.

Chase quickly turned his good side to Riley and clapped an arm around his waist.

"You won!" Riley beamed.

"I won," Chase confirmed. "You want to see?" He handed the belt buckle to Riley in order to distract him, then he met Maddy's gaze over his head.

She gave him a helpless expression. It was clear she was at a loss on how to handle the problem.

"Are you okay?" she asked. "Your ribs?"

"Took another hit," he admitted.

Her expression turned immediately to concern.

"But don't worry," he quickly added. "I'll be dancing at the party."

Riley instantly perked up. "Party? Are we goin' to a party?"

"It's for the bull riders," Maddy told her son.

"Daddy's a bull rider."

Maddy didn't seem to know how to respond.

"Can we go for a little while?" Riley asked. "Is there candy?"

"Cupcakes," Zane said.

Maddy gave her brother a look of annoyance.

"The kid can have a cupcake," Zane said.

"It's two hours past his bedtime."

"He can sleep in the car on the way home, Matilda."

Maddy rolled her eyes at her brother, but then she looked down at Riley, who was still clinging to Chase's leg.

Her gaze softened on her son. "One cupcake."

"Will Daddy drive us home?" Riley asked, his grip tightening.

It was clear he was afraid Chase would be taken away from him. Chase wondered if, deep down, Riley knew Chase wasn't his father, and the jig would soon be up. Or maybe it was because his father had been gone for such a long time, and he was worried it would happen again. It was hard to guess what went on inside the head of a three-year-old.

"We have our own car," Maddy said.

Riley's face screwed up in a pout. "I wanna drive with Daddy."

"One more complaint," Maddy told him in a sharper tone, "and we'll skip the cupcake altogether."

Riley compressed his lips. He still looked sullen, but he wasn't about to complain and lose out on the cupcake. Chase couldn't help but be impressed by that level of control from a little kid.

RILEY'S HALF EATEN cupcake was on the table next to where Chase held him in his arms. Her son's eyes were closed. His head was on Chase's shoulder, his knees on Chase's lap, and Chase's arm held him fast to his chest.

"You're in pain," Maddy said to Chase, feeling regret and gratitude in equal measures.

"It's not too bad," he responded, though the tightness around his mouth said otherwise.

"This has gone on long enough," she said, rising and reaching out to take Riley.

Chase had already gone above and beyond the call of duty. And it was her fault he'd gotten injured in the first place. It was obvious he wanted nothing more than to lie down in a bed somewhere and go unconscious for a while.

"He's almost out," Chase told her in an undertone. "Give him a couple of minutes."

"Why are you doing this?" She stayed at the ready.

"He seems like a good kid." Chase made no move to hand him over.

"His is a good kid. But that doesn't mean you have to be a saint."

Chase grinned. "Nobody's ever called me that before."

"They should have." She found herself caught all over again by his compelling eyes.

They were slate gray in the dim light, an odd combination of familiar and mysterious. His brow was dark, nose straight, and his chin was square, covered in raw stubble. His lips were fuller than her husband's, but the quirky smile was the same.

His eyes went opaque, and she realized he was scrutinizing her the same way she was scrutinizing him. The untamed energy seemed to rise between them again.

"What *do* they call you?" she asked, grasping at the last thread of their conversation, realizing she was being rapidly drawn in by her attraction to him.

His expression tightened. "Rash, wild, volatile, and irresponsible."

"You're warning me off."

He didn't deny it.

"Why would you do that?" she asked.

"Reflex, mostly. I warn off all the nice girls that seem interested in me."

"I can see you have a pretty high opinion of yourself."

"Maybe." He might have been joking, but it was hard to tell.

"I'm not coming on to you." She felt the need to clarify.

At least, she wasn't doing it on purpose. Were her emotions that transparent?

"I'm glad to hear it," Chase said. "He's asleep, by the

way."

Maddy fought off a rising sense of embarrassment. She hadn't intended to flirt. Sure, she found Chase unaccountably sexy. And it seemed likely that other women did too. But she didn't think she'd said or done anything to give herself away.

"Hey, little sister." Zane's voice was tipsy jovial as he wrapped an arm around her shoulders.

"I can see you've been enjoying yourself," she said, grateful to him for the interruption.

Zane peered at Chase. "You need a shot?"

"Next on my list," Chase drawled. "Didn't want to babysit under the influence."

"You haven't even had a drink?" Maddy was feeling worse and worse about Riley clinging to Chase.

If anybody deserved a stiff shot, it was the night's winner, who also happened to be in pain from his injury.

"Let me get you something," she quickly offered.

"I'll go," Zane said.

"No. Stay here. Maybe take Riley so Chase can rest." She was happy to take the excuse to get away. Chase was far too perceptive for her comfort.

"Sure." Zane set down his glass and staggered sideways a step.

"Yeah, I don't think so," Chase said to Zane. To Maddy, he said, "Any whiskey they've got, neat. Make it a double."

Weaving her way between tables and revelers, she made

her way to the bar across the room.

She had to get her emotions under control. She had no business being attracted to Chase. The situation was complicated enough.

"A double whiskey," she told the bartender when her turn came in the lineup.

"You got an ID?" the man asked.

Maddy realized she didn't. She had a credit card, some cash, and her AEBR ticket in her jeans pocket, but that was it.

"Not with me," she told him.

"Sorry, honey."

"I've over twenty-one."

"I'm sure you are. But unless you can prove it to me, I can't serve you."

"But—"

He looked over her shoulder to the next customer. "Can I help you, sir?"

She clamped her jaw in annoyance. She was going to have to send Zane to buy the drinks. He was only seven minutes older, but he hadn't been carded since he was eighteen.

Accepting defeat, she pushed away from the bar, retracing her steps to where Zane was sharing some kind of a story with Chase.

Chase looked at her empty hands.

"No ID," she said.

Zane burst out laughing, and she gave him a punch in the shoulder.

"How old are you?" Chase asked, glancing at Riley then narrowing his gaze on Maddy.

"Twenty-two," said Zane. "We're the same age."

"Twins?" Chase asked.

"Go get the man a whisky," she told her brother.

"Never get carded," Zane bragged, voice cocky as he backed away.

"He do that to you often?" Chase asked.

"All the time."

"You do look younger than him."

Maddy sat down on the bench next to Chase. "I'm sure I'll thank you for that someday."

"But not today?"

"Not today." She put out her arms to take Riley.

Chase didn't hand him over, and there was humor in his tone when he spoke. "You wouldn't expect a guy to have this much trouble getting a shot of whisky at an AEBR event."

"I'll take him," she said.

"He's fine."

"I'll take him," she repeated, reaching for Riley.

Chase presented her with his shoulder. "We don't want to wake him."

"We won't."

"I like holding him."

"No you don't. You're being chivalrous."

"I told you, I'm rash, wild, volatile, and irresponsible."

"You lied about that," she said.

"Ask anyone. So, you're twenty-two?"

"I am." She gave up and let her arms drop.

"You were nineteen when you had Riley?"

"Congratulations. You can do arithmetic."

"Eighteen when you got pregnant."

"*And* got married." She didn't know why she felt it necessary to emphasize the wedding. It wasn't like any woman had to defend her virtue in this day and age.

"In that order?" he asked.

"What's your point?"

"My point is Chase Barrett should have kept his hands to himself."

"You realize you're criticizing my dead husband?"

Chase's jaw clamped shut, and his expression shuttered. "I'm sorry. That was dead wrong of me."

Maddy wasn't sure how to react. Chase had absolutely been out of line. But he wasn't wrong. She'd been young and naive when she met Chase Barrett. He'd been older and a whole lot more worldly. He'd sworn up and down that he loved her. But things had raced way beyond her control before she'd known what was happening.

She tried to lighten the conversation. "Since you saved my son's life, I suppose I can give you a pass."

"You shouldn't. Give me a pass, I mean. You should slap me or something." He looked prepared to take whatever she dished out.

"You're injured." She had absolutely no desire to physically hurt him.

"Well, don't slap me in the ribs."

She couldn't help but smile. "I'm not going to slap you anywhere."

Their gazes caught and held. She sobered again. She didn't want to slap him. She wanted to kiss him. She suddenly realized she very desperately wanted to kiss him. She hadn't felt that way in a very, very long time.

Zane arrived. "Two shots of whisky, as ordered," he announced in a jovial voice.

Chase took one of them with his free hand.

Maddy pointed to the other. "Do you mind?"

"Be my guest," Chase said.

She took the shot from Zane and downed it.

CHASE'S INJURIES WERE significant. Being in pain was nothing new. He got scrapes, bruises and worse all the time, and rode anyway. But even before the doctor had confirmed late last night that he had three broken ribs, Chase had known he was going to be out of commission for a while.

It wasn't the end of the world. He'd joined the AEBR tour partway into the season, so he wasn't in the running for overall points. And he wasn't riding for the money. He was riding to stay on the road and to keep his memories of Laura-Leigh and Patrick at bay.

So he didn't want to slow down, and he sure didn't want to stop. Deadwood was a quiet town between events. He'd have way too much time on his hands. And he absolutely hated the thought of being cooped up with nothing but his own thoughts.

It was eight a.m. and he levered himself out of the motel room bed, carefully pulling on a pair of jeans and a fresh T-shirt. He'd seen a café a couple of doors down. Coffee and pancakes sounded good.

A knock sounded on the door, and he moved on bare feet to answer it.

To his surprise, it was Zane Merrick.

"Mornin'," Chase greeted. "I thought you'd be on the road by now."

"It's only five hours to Billings. I'm not in any big rush. And it's good to be home for a few days."

"You live here?" Chase supposed that made sense, given Zane had a sister and a nephew in town.

His thoughts returned to the lovely Maddy, remembering the attraction that had built up over the course of the evening. By the time she'd taken her sleeping son and left for home, Chase had been ready to drag her into his arms and kiss her senseless. Now, he gave himself a shake, reminding himself he was talking to her brother.

"My family used to have a spread up in the valley. Long

story in that. But the spread's gone. Maddy's the only one left there now. We kept a small parcel with the house."

"How's she doing today?"

Zane gave him an odd look, and Chase worried the question might have given away his attraction to her.

"I meant with Riley. Is he over whatever he had going on last night?"

"You mean is he over being convinced you were his father?"

"That's what I mean."

Zane shook his head. "You were the first thing he asked about this morning. He rushed into Maddy's bedroom, expecting to find you there."

Chase swore softly.

"I came to bring you this." Zane held out the buckle Chase had won last night.

"I don't need it." Chase couldn't help but wonder if Riley might have liked to keep it. Would it make him feel better? Or would it perpetuate his fantasy and maybe slow down his acceptance of reality?

He decided it was probably better if Riley didn't have any reminders of last night.

So Chase accepted the buckle, feeling unaccountably let down. "Thanks."

Zane didn't leave.

"You want to come in?" Chase asked.

Zane's gaze narrowed in obvious contemplation.

"You got something to say to me?"

Chase couldn't help but wonder if Zane had figured out that he was attracted to his sister. He hadn't done a single thing about it except to think about her. And a guy couldn't be condemned for his thoughts, although it was better if Zane didn't know about those thoughts. Chase had thought about her a whole lot, especially last night when every breath he took hurt. Imagining her in his arms was a balm to his pain.

Maybe this was Zane trying to warn him off. Chase wouldn't blame the man for doing that.

"I'm trying to decide," Zane began, "if seeing more of you is better than seeing less of you."

"You mean for Riley," Chase guessed.

"Who else?"

"Nobody."

There was no way it was good for Maddy to see more of Chase. It might be nice for him to see more of her. But that was selfishness talking.

"If he doesn't figure it out for himself, if you leave while this fantasy is still fixed in his brain, he might keep believing you're him," Zane said.

"And he'll think his dad abandoned him all over again." Chase understood Zane's worry.

Zane nodded.

"What does Maddy think?"

"She just wants it all to go away."

Chase couldn't blame her for that. "Riley's mama could be right."

For Chase to disappear right away could be the best way to handle the problem.

"I think she's wrong," Zane said.

"I'm not going to impose myself on them."

"He's my nephew, and I love him."

"She's his mother, and it's her job to protect him."

"Mothers don't always know best."

Chase couldn't disagree with that. His own mother made more mistakes then he could count raising him. Erratic and self-centered, she certainly wasn't the model for child-rearing. But Maddy didn't strike him as being anything remotely like his mother.

"Why don't you let me worry about my sister?" Zane said.

"Do I really look that much like him?" Chase couldn't help but be curious.

"There are pictures at the house." Zane's manipulation was pretty obvious.

"I'm not that curious."

Zane cocked his head. "He was shorter, slighter than you. I think it's the eyes, the nose, and something about your expression. Stills side-by-side would be fairly startling, but you'd know it was two different men. Thing is, when you start talking and smiling, or especially frowning, it's like you could be his brother. I think Riley saw you from afar and wanted desperately to believe."

The supposition made sense to Chase. It seemed likely that it was exactly what happened.

"You're banking that he'll figure it out on his own if he sees more of me."

"We can reinforce that you're a nice man who looks a lot like his father."

"A nice man?"

Nobody had ever described Chase like that before. When they were looking for a compliment, they'd say he was hard-working, maybe quiet, but never nice.

"He needs to see it for himself," Zane said. "I'm convinced that's the only way he'll get over you. He was in tears when I left the house this morning. He blames Maddy for sending you away."

That knowledge hit Chase hard. Maddy didn't deserve her son's anger. She seemed like a wonderful mother, and a genuinely caring human being. Not to mention smart and sexy. Not that her being smart and sexy had anything to do with his decision. Still…

She'd obviously been dealt some blows in life. He could relate to that, and he was willing to step in and help if he could.

"We can't have him blaming Maddy," Chase said.

At the very least, Chase could take the blame on his own shoulders. When he left, if Riley still believed he was his father, then Chase would take the blame himself. He'd be sure to absolve Maddy.

Mind made up, he stepped into his boots. "Let's go."

"You had breakfast?" Zane asked.

"It can wait."

"Maddy makes fantastic pancakes."

Chase couldn't help but smile. "You don't need to bribe me. I've already said yes."

"It's not a bribe. It's a reward," Zane said, opening the motel room door. "For good behavior."

Chase laughed, then groaned, laying his arm protectively across his ribs.

"Been there, done that," Zane said sympathetically as they stepped onto the sidewalk that bordered the motel parking lot.

It was hot outside, with heat waves from the morning sun shimmering off the asphalt. Cars whizzed by on the highway, while tourists in colorful T-shirts and flip flops waited for the shuttle bus to take them to the shopping district downtown.

"Billings?" Zane asked, obviously wondering if Chase would compete next weekend.

"The doc's afraid I'll puncture a lung."

"That's what ended Chet Donavan's career."

"I can live with missing Billings," Chase said. "I can't live with tanking my career altogether."

"Amen to that."

Chapter Three

MADDY COULDN'T BELIEVE her eyes.

"Daddy!" Riley cried out, launching himself across the living room to throw himself in Chase's arms.

"What are you doing here?" she hissed over her son's head.

Riley buried his face in Chase's shoulder as soon as Chase lifted him off the ground.

She glared at Zane who walked in behind Chase. It was obvious what had happened.

"He's here to help, Matilda," Zane said in an undertone, moving closer to her.

"I finally got him to calm down." She couldn't imagine how feeding Riley's fantasy could be expected to help.

"How're you doing, buckaroo?" Chase asked.

"Good, Daddy, good." Riley gave an eager nod. "Do you want to see my monster truck? I got it for Christmas. It's green and yellow, and it has a big ol' *skull* on the front."

Chase set Riley carefully down on the carpet, obviously protecting his ribs with every move. "I'd love to see your monster truck." His gaze met Maddy's.

She glared at him, attempting to silently convey her anger. As soon as he left, she was going to have to start all over again with Riley.

"Why don't you go get it?" Chase asked her son.

"Sure," Riley readily agreed, taking off down the hall at a trot.

She lifted her hands in helplessness. "I don't understand. What are you two *thinking*?"

Chase stepped forward. "Zane says he blames you. He said Riley thought you sent me away."

"I didn't *send you away*. You were never here in the first place."

"You know what I mean."

"What I don't know is how you think this will help. It's only going to confuse him more."

"I'll tell him the truth," Chase said.

"You don't think I've been telling him the truth?" She struggled to keep her voice down. "He refuses to believe it."

"Maybe coming from me—"

"Instead of *his mother*?" She was angry with Chase, but she realized she was even angrier with her brother.

"Why did you bring him?" she demanded of Zane.

"There are differences," Zane said.

"Obviously." She found herself looking back at Chase.

There were startling similarities, but there were significant differences in the two men's looks as well as their personalities.

This Chase was more laid back, slower talking, with a base-line sense of humor she'd never seen in her husband. Her husband was more tightly wound, faster to speak, faster to move, with an edginess that made him seem uber-alert, like he was constantly ready to defend himself. This Chase, on the other hand, acted like there was nothing to defend, nothing to really worry about.

She realized she was the one on edge here. She had good reason, but maybe it wasn't helping. It was regrettable that he'd shown up again. But the damage was done. There was nothing she could so right now to fundamentally change the circumstances.

Riley once again thought his father had come home. She couldn't go back in time and stop it, so she was going to have to figure out how to deal with it.

"If it doesn't work," Chase said. "If I can't get him to see reality. Then when I leave, I'll make sure he doesn't blame you."

When she looked into his silver-gray eyes, she saw sincerity. He genuinely believed he was here to help. She was more than a little skeptical that it would work. But she found some of her anger dissipating.

"Here it is." Riley's voice echoed down the hall, his running footsteps coming toward them.

He hugged a huge, plastic monster truck to his chest. It had been his favorite Christmas present.

Zane had helped her pick it out. He'd also helped pay for

it, since Chase's life insurance policy had been modest, and her budget was very tight. Maddy had already made a few inquiries about getting a job, even though it was difficult to think of leaving Riley with a sitter or at a daycare.

Chase crouched on his haunches. "That's a pretty great truck."

"I got it for Christmas."

"From Santa?"

Riley nodded, his eyes alight with excitement. "It came with batteries. Mom put them inside." He pointed to the battery compartment cover, sliding it open to show Chase. "It climbs all the way up the driveway."

"Are they rechargeable?" Chase asked.

"Yes. The charger is in my bedroom." Information poured out of Riley. It was as if he was making up for lost time. "I put them in there every night. I also have a bike. It has training wheels. But when I turn four, I'm going to learn to ride it without. Will you be here then?"

Riley's earnest expression nearly broke Maddy's heart.

"Why don't you show me how your truck works?" Chase asked.

"It has a remote." Riley removed the remote control from where he'd stowed it in the pickup box.

The sound of the motor filled the room, while the lights on the truck came to life, and he sent it across the kitchen floor and onto the carpet. Riley and Chase moved to follow the progress.

"It's going to be okay," Zane told her in a low voice.

"It's not going to be okay." She blinked hard. "Best case scenario, we get him to understand death and his little heart gets broken all over again."

Zane wrapped a strong arm around her shoulders. "I hate to agree, but that's true."

Maddy sniffed back her tears, refusing to let them fall. She'd cried enough over this for a lifetime. It wasn't fair that Riley had lost his father. But there was no way for her to change that.

"Are you hungry?" she asked Zane, gathering her resolve.

"You got pancakes?"

"I can make some."

"If you don't mind."

"I don't mind."

She'd already cleaned up after hers and Riley's breakfast, but it was better for her to keep busy today.

"I hauled Chase out of bed," Zane said. "I imagine he's hungry too."

"Hung over?"

Chase hadn't seemed to drink much last night. But she left the party before he did, so who knew what had happened after that? She'd certainly seen plenty of buckle winners celebrate into the wee hours of the morning.

"Three broken ribs."

"Ouch." It wasn't a huge surprise, but her sympathies definitely went out to him.

"He'll have to skip Billings."

Maddy knew how important it was for the riders to post scores at every opportunity. Competition was fierce for the overall title. She couldn't imagine Chase would be happy about missing an event. Then she felt guilty all over again. If he hadn't saved Riley, he wouldn't have suffered the initial injury. And it was likely the second fall from the finals bull would have resulted in nothing more than bruises.

"You want blueberries?" she asked her brother.

Zane grinned. "I'll take 'em."

"I'm still mad at you."

"You'll get over it. You always do."

Riley's voice was clear in the kitchen as he spoke above the truck's sound. "It always gets caught there."

Maddy couldn't help but glance into the other room. As she suspected, Riley was talking about the torn corner of her carpet. She felt a flash of embarrassment over its condition. Her floors all needed replacing, but she didn't have the money to hire installers, and she didn't have the expertise to do it herself.

Her brothers would help her if she asked, but Zane was in the midst of the bull-riding season. Her oldest brother Lucas had long since moved to New York City. Her middle brothers Eli and Wyatt were both struggling to earn as much money as they could, while trying to find a loophole in a lien agreement in order to get the family's land back. The carpets might be embarrassing, but replacing them was optional not mandatory.

"Have you got a basement?" Chase asked Riley.

Riley gave him an odd look. "You don't remember the basement?"

"There are a lot of things around here that are new to me," Chase said.

"You want to see my bike?" Riley asked. "It's down there right now."

"I'd love to see your bike." Chase flipped the switch to turn off the truck. "Show me the way."

"You've gotta think," Zane said, "that a guy like that has a lot better things to do than humor a three-year-old."

Maddy had to admit it was probably true. "So why did you drag him here?"

"For Riley," Zane said. "For you."

"Are you making a point?"

"I'm trying to get you to adjust your attitude. Chase isn't the bad guy."

"So, *you're* the bad guy?"

She wished her stomach would stop churning. But she couldn't shake a feeling of dread. They were playing with fire here, teetering on the edge of Riley's psyche.

"There is no bad guy," Zane said.

"Then why is everything so messed up?" She took a mixing bowl from a bottom shelf and placed it on the counter.

There should be a bad guy. It would be nice to have someone to blame for the situation, someone besides herself, since she was the one who should have noticed Riley didn't understand that his father's death meant he was never coming back. How had she missed that?

She pulled out the flour canister and scooped a couple of cups into the bowl.

"Because bad things happen to good people," Zane said.

"They should stop." She added salt.

"They will."

She gripped the lip of the counter. "Quit being so philosophical."

Zane moved closer. "What do you want me to be?"

"I don't know." She honestly didn't. "Can I go to sleep now and have somebody wake me when this is all over?"

His voice was soft. "When what's all over?"

"When Riley is back to normal and Chase Garrett is gone."

"Sure," Zane said, there was a thread of humor in his voice. "Well, as soon as you've finished making the pancakes."

"You know how to make pancakes."

"You make them better."

"Food always tastes better when you're not the one who cooks it."

"Is that true?"

"Yes."

"You cook all the time."

"That's how I stay thin."

Zane laughed at that. "And here I thought it was because you worked so hard."

"That too."

She did work hard. Taking care of a house all alone was hard, especially an old house on a big property, especially when a woman didn't have much of a repair budget. It was hard, and she was tired, but she was all Riley had, and she didn't have time to rest.

CHASE HAD FOUND what he was looking for in the basement. Then he'd dug into Maddy's blueberry pancakes, amazed by how good they tasted. Zane hadn't oversold them in the least.

Now, hours later, he was in the backyard of the white, single story farmhouse. Riley was playing on a swing set and Zane was saying goodbye to his sister before heading out to meet some friends from the AEBR circuit who were still in town. They'd grilled hotdogs for dinner, and Chase had easily agreed to stick around until Riley's bedtime. He liked Maddy a whole lot, and Riley was a great kid. And hanging out with them kept his mind focused in the present.

"Look at me!" Riley called as he pumped himself higher on the swing.

"Hang on tight," Chase called across the yard.

"Be careful," Maddy warned as she joined Chase at the

weathered picnic table.

He was sitting on top, with his feet planted on the bench.

She climbed up beside him.

The sun was heading down behind the distant mountains, the shadows long across the sun-warmed grass. That grass badly needed mowing. The fence needed painting, and the gravel driveway was being invaded by weeds.

"You have a nice view," he said.

"We used to own all of that." She swept her arm across the vista of rolling rangeland hills dotted with Herefords.

"What happened?"

"My father borrowed a lot of money before he died. Nobody fully understood the terms of the loan. The creditor held back information, so when things got tight we lost the land to him."

Chase would have liked more details. It sounded like the family had somehow got a raw deal. But he didn't want to pry. "I'm sorry to hear that."

"Lucas, Eli, and Wyatt, my other brothers, want it back. But they don't have the money."

"Have you given up?"

Chase didn't think he'd be so sanguine about giving up his land. Then again, he'd walked away from his land, and he had no intention of ever going back. He supposed he might as well sell it. Right now, it was leased out. That way his options were open. If he ever had children—

He stopped that thought in its tracks. After Laura-Leigh, he doubted he'd ever trust another woman, never mind let himself fall in love with one and marry her. And he couldn't see himself as a single father. His gaze rested on Riley. His hat was off to Maddy for the job she was doing here.

"Was this the original house?" he asked, to keep the conversation going.

She shaded her eyes to look. "Five kids in three bedrooms when we were young. I was the only girl, so I got my own room. More of a closet, really. Lucas and Eli slept in the basement. One bathroom, though. That was a challenge."

"It seems like a good size for the two of you."

"It is."

They fell to silence, watching Riley.

"He's not figuring it out," she said softly.

Chase shifted his seat. "I know. I keep pointing to things that are new to me, and he insists I've forgotten. I haven't wanted to say it head-on."

"I did. This morning."

"What did you say?"

"I told him you were a nice man that looked like Daddy, but you weren't his daddy."

"You called me nice?" There was something soft in his expression as he said it.

"*That's* what you took from that?"

"It's the second time today."

"Is that unusual?" she asked.

"It's also the second time ever."

She tipped her head as she looked at him. "Nobody's ever called you nice before?"

The sun glowed on her fresh face, and she looked angelic as she smiled.

"I'm not," he said.

"You seem plenty nice to me, Chase Garrett. You just spent an entire day humoring my confused son."

"You caught me in a weakened state. And I didn't have anything better to do. This kept my mind from wandering."

"Wandering where?"

"It doesn't matter. I hope I can help."

Her smile disappeared. "Me too."

"I made you stop smiling. I didn't mean to do that."

"I just remembered why you were here. And that it's my fault you got hurt."

"Maddy." He had to check an impulse to reach for her hand.

He wanted to reassure her it wasn't in any way her fault. Injuries happened in bull riding. It was the nature of the sport.

But she stepped down from the table. "Riley, time to get ready for bed."

Riley gave a mighty push and jumped off the swing, coming down on all fours in the dust. "I want Daddy to tuck me in."

"There'll be no tucking before you take a bath. You're

filthy."

"It's good Montana dirt," Riley said, quoting his uncle Zane again.

"We still need to wash it off." She held out her hand to him.

"Daddy can give me my bath."

"Chase doesn't need to bathe you."

Riley stopped dead, his lips compressing. "You give me a bath *all* the time."

"That's because I'm your mother."

Chase didn't know whether to step in or stay silent. He'd be happy to help Riley with a bath, but he didn't want to undermine Maddy.

"It's Daddy's turn."

"Riley." There was a warning tone in Maddy's voice.

Chase could see a standoff coming. He'd known little boys. He'd been a little boy, and this was about to get ugly.

"How about this?" he said, coming to his feet. "Your mommy gives you a bath, but I'll read you both a story while she does."

Maddy shot him an unfathomable look. He couldn't tell if she was relieved or annoyed.

"A story!" Riley shouted, skipping forward again. "I want the *Little Red Train*." He let go of Maddy's hand and barreled for the door.

"I hope that's okay," Chase said to her.

She looked straight ahead as she walked.

CHASE

He fell into step. "Maddy?"

"I don't know," she answered. "It feels like I should be mad because you interfered. But I'm relieved. It's embarrassing to say that. A good mother would have stuck to her guns."

"You did stick to your guns."

"Only because you switched the target."

He tried to wrap his head around the metaphor. "Okay, I don't really know what that means. But Riley's skipping toward the bathtub instead of taking a tantrum on the back lawn. I'm going to take that as a win."

They took the few wooden steps to the back porch.

She stopped and he stopped with her.

She turned to look at him, her face shadowed, her hair billowing in the breeze. Her blue eyes were as bright as ever. And even in this light he could see her cute freckles.

"Why did you come back?" she asked.

He wasn't sure how to answer that question, so he went for the obvious. "Because Zane asked me."

She searched his expression. "Most men would have said no."

"I guess I'm not most men." He wanted to kiss her so badly.

Her voice went softer still. "I'm afraid you might be making things worse."

"So am I," he admitted.

She eased in and the air emptied from his lungs. He held

63

himself steady with an iron will.

"Chase?" Her voice was breathless.

"Yes?" His was the same.

"It's been forever since a man kissed me."

He didn't need a second invitation. He bent down, pressing his lips to hers and gently gripped her shoulders. Her lips parted. Her head tilted to meet him. And she kissed him back.

Her response was fuel to his fire. He wrapped his arms around her. He pressed the length of her against him, feeling the softness of her curves cradle his hard body. She felt good, so, so good.

"Daddy, I found *Little Red Train*."

Riley appeared in the doorway and they jumped guiltily apart.

Chase's ribs shot through with pain, but he couldn't have cared less.

Riley waved a picture book. "It was under my bed. We tore one of the pages before, but Mommy taped it."

"That's good, buckaroo." Chase looked into Maddy's eyes, steeling himself to see her regret.

But there was no regret. He saw surprise and confusion. Her eyes were midnight blue, her red lips slightly swollen, and her cheeks were flushed with color. But there was no regret. He breathed a sigh of relief.

"You okay?" he asked her softly.

He got a shaky nod in return, while Riley grasped onto

his leg. "We can do the choo-choo sound."

Chase raised a brow to Maddy.

"We all do the whistle sound together when the train goes up the hill."

"Okay," Chase agreed, carefully lifting Riley on his good side. "We'll do the choo-choo sound."

CHASE WOKE UP disoriented and in pain. At first, he thought he was in his motel room. But then he remembered reading the train book, having a beer with Maddy after Riley fell asleep, then popping a pain pill while he waited for Zane to return and give him a lift back to town. He realized he must have fallen asleep on Maddy's sofa.

A shaft of light from her front porch filtered through the front drapes, outlining an easy chair and the table lamp. He was covered in a blanket. His toes had gone numb, and his legs were cramped from being bent against the arm of the sofa. But his ribs were the worst. For a moment, he was afraid to move.

But then he took a bracing breath, grasped the back of the sofa and pulled himself into a sitting position. He bit back a moan, struggling to remember where he'd put the pain pills.

"You okay?" Maddy asked.

He blinked and she came into focus, a shadow moving

from the hallway into the living room.

"What time is it?" he asked.

"About three."

"And you're still up?"

"I heard you moan in your sleep."

"I'm sorry." He hated that she was seeing him in a moment of weakness.

"Your ribs are broken. I think that's a pretty good excuse."

"Did you see where I put the pills?"

"Can I turn on the light?"

"Go ahead. You didn't undress me or anything?" He put a hand to his chest and found he was wearing his T-shirt.

"You wish." She clicked on a small lamp on the far side of the room.

"I do," he said before thinking better of it.

Sure, they'd shared a kiss. And it was one hell of a kiss, but he didn't want to embarrass her.

"The pills are on the table next to you."

He couldn't tell if she was annoyed by his remark or not.

"Did Zane make it home?" he asked, moving on.

"Not yet." She was wearing a gray T-shirt and a set of green plaid pajama bottoms.

Chase had to force himself to look away. "Is that unusual?" He opened the small bottle and shook two of the yellow pills into his palm.

"Not at all. You know bull riders. There are poker games

and buckle bunnies, no end to the trouble or fun, depending on how you look at it."

"I suppose." Chase had had his share of offers over the past few months. He'd said no to them all, but plenty of single riders had casual dates in the towns along the circuit.

"Water?" she asked.

"I can get it." He tried to stand, but pain burned through his chest.

"Don't be ridiculous." She headed for the kitchen.

He watched her walk away, thinking she had about the hottest body he'd ever seen. The curve of her waist and the strip of bare skin made the T-shirt and low-riding bottoms sexier than any silk negligee.

She disappeared and he heard the tap running.

"It's been five hours since you took the last pill," she called back to him.

That explained why he felt so crappy. The doctor had warned him to keep the dosage up for a couple of days.

"They're okay to take every four hours," he said as she walked back into the room.

This time, his view was her front. One glance at her rounded breasts, and he was imagining them in the palm of his hands.

She sat down next to him and handed over the glass of water. "Here you go."

He silently ordered himself to keep his eyes front. "I don't expect you to be my nurse."

"It's no trouble."

"Thank you."

"Swallow your pills."

"Yes, ma'am." He tossed them to the back of his throat.

"You can't be comfortable out here," she said.

He nearly choked on the pills. There was no way in the world she was suggesting he share her bed. But that was the first place his wayward mind went.

"Take Zane's bed," she continued. "It's his fault you can't get back to the motel."

Chase coughed, struggling to recover, and then he swallowed. "I'm fine."

"I'm serious. If he gets home, he can sleep out here."

"I'm not taking the man's bed."

"You're injured, and you're here helping me out. I'm not forcing you to sleep on a lumpy, old couch."

"It's not lumpy."

"It's short, and you're tall," she said. She rose to her feet. "Come on."

"You're going to tuck me in?" Again, as soon as the words were out, he regretted them. "I'm sorry. That was out of line."

"I did kiss you."

He was surprised that she'd so casually tossed that out on the table. "What are you saying?"

"I'm saying, I kissed you, and you're allowed to make a joke."

He rose beside her, careful to keep the pain out of his expression. He didn't want her pity.

"I'm still sorry. Because it wasn't a joke." He paused. "Okay, it was half a joke. But a guy can hope for a long shot."

"And what were you going to do if I'd said yes?" She looked pointedly at his injured ribs.

"Where there's a will, there's a way." He was lying. He could barely breathe. He wasn't anybody's dream lover in this condition.

She chuckled. "I admire your spirit, cowboy."

"You're mocking me."

"I'm mocking you. And I'm putting you to bed. Alone. So that you can recover."

"And after I recover?"

She shook her head and made a clicking sound with her cheek. "You're putting way too much on one kiss."

"It was a great kiss."

She started for the hallway. "It was a spur of the moment thing."

"It seemed like you liked it." He followed, not because he cared so much about sleeping in a real bed, but because he didn't want their conversation to end.

"I thought it was—"

Riley's voice interrupted. "No!" he cried out.

Maddy's expression instantly changed. She rushed down the hall. Of necessity, Chase moved more slowly behind her.

"Stop," Riley cried. "Mama!"

"It's okay, sweetheart," Maddy crooned as she crossed into the bedroom to Riley's bedside.

Chase came to a stop in the doorway, unsure of what to do.

In the dim glow from a nightlight, Riley was sitting up in his bed. His eyes were wide, but he didn't look to be awake.

She sat down on the red and yellow quilt, putting an arm around his little shoulders and smoothing his hair. "You had a bad dream."

Riley recoiled. "Stop! Stop!"

"Wake up, honey," Maddy said.

Chase took a reflexive step into the room.

"Daddy, no!" Riley flailed his little arms.

Chase moved closer, wanting to do something. "Has this happened before?"

"Not for months," she said, a quaver in her voice. "Wake up, Riley."

"It's going to eat him," Riley wailed.

Maddy gave her son a little shake. "It's only a dream. You can wake up now."

Riley looked at Maddy. This time, he seemed to be conscious. He swallowed.

"The bull was eating Daddy," he said.

Chase sat down on the end of the bed, his heart contracting at the fear in Riley's voice. He struggled to think of how to help.

"Bulls only eat grass," he offered calmly.

Riley's attention flew to him. In an instant, he was launching himself at Chase.

Chase turned just in time to protect his injured left side. He wrapped his right arm around Riley to hold him steady.

"You're not dead," Riley said.

Chase's stomach turned to a block of cement. He met Maddy's horrified gaze, and it took him a moment to find his voice.

"It was just a bad dream," he told Riley, hoping it was the right thing to say.

"He was big and black, and snot was running out of his nose. He had horns. And his eyes were red, red like the Devil."

"Riley." Chase drew back. "It's over now. There's no bull."

Riley's lower lip quivered. "He was eating you."

Chase was at a loss. He knew he should give Riley back to his mother. But he couldn't bring himself to push the frightened, clinging boy away. But he also couldn't perpetuate Riley's delusion that he was his father.

"I hope I was delicious," he said.

Maddy looked stunned.

But Riley drew back, blinking up at Chase.

Chase gave him a grin and ruffled his hair. "The bull must have been awfully hungry. Because I'm a tough old thing. I bet some tasty, tender blue grass would have been way better."

"That's silly," said Riley, but his tears were drying.

"What's silly is a bull wanting to snack on a cowboy. Your dream was just as crazy as mine."

"You had a dream?" Riley asked.

"I did."

"Tonight?"

"Yes." Chase was making this up as he went along.

"Did it have a bull?"

"No. It had a pretty little heifer. She was black and white, and she was eating marshmallows."

Riley grinned, and even Maddy seemed to be fighting a smile.

"Big, gooey marshmallows." Chase was making it up on the fly.

"I like marshmallows."

"So do I," Chase said. "I toast 'em over an open fire until they're crispy brown on the outside and warm and runny on the inside."

Riley looked at Maddy. "Mommy, I'm hungry."

"You can't have marshmallows in the middle of the night," Maddy said, surreptitiously wiping her cheeks with the back of her hand. "You'll get a stomach ache."

"Can I have a glass of water?"

"Yes, you can have a glass of water."

"I'll get it," Chase said.

Riley seemed to hesitate.

"You let your mommy tuck you back into bed."

It took a moment, but then Riley nodded. "Yes, sir."

"Good man," Chase said, easing Riley back into his mother's arms.

"Can I have marshmallows tomorrow?"

"We'll see," Maddy said.

Chase rose from the bed, feeling strangely shaken. As he moved, his pain came back in force. He struggled to walk straight until he was out of Maddy's sight. And then he bent protectively over his ribs, making his way slowly to the kitchen sink.

When he returned, Riley was already asleep.

"He went back to sleep easier than I expected," Chase said, setting the glass of water on the bedside table.

"Thank you for that," Maddy said, stroking her hand over Riley's forehead.

"I'm not sure I helped." It probably would have been better overall if he'd stayed outside in the hallway. "I'm afraid I've made things worse."

"Right after my husband... Right after Riley's father died, Riley used to have nightmares."

"Was there always a bull in them?" Chase wondered if anyone had told Riley that a bull killed his father. But he didn't want to ask.

"It used to be random monsters, sometimes wolves or bears."

"So he doesn't know?"

"That his father was killed by a bull? No, he doesn't know that."

"Then this is probably about last night."

Maddy gave a nod as she rose to her feet. "I expect it was."

"Understandable. And likely temporary." Chase couldn't help but feel relieved. If the nightmare was connected to Riley falling into the ring, it *was* likely temporary.

Chase would hate to think his presence had brought back something more deeply seated in Riley's psyche related to his father's death. The last thing he wanted to do was hurt Riley. Or hurt Maddy. He'd hate it if he hurt Maddy.

Chapter Four

MADDY HAD NO idea what to make of Chase Garrett. It was morning now, and she knew things had to get back to normal. Riley had to stop pretending Chase was his father, and Maddy had to stop fantasizing about the man.

The kiss on the porch had stuck with her. If not for Riley's nightmare, she wasn't sure what she might have done in the middle of the night. Chase had looked rumpled and sexy on her sofa. She'd be lying to pretend her fantasies hadn't gone beyond kissing. She was a normal, healthy woman, and her husband had been gone now for months.

Truth be told, her husband had checked out of their relationship long before that fateful night. In fact, if not for her pregnancy with Riley, they might never have gotten married at all. But they had gotten married, and she at least had been faithful.

The front door opened, and Zane appeared, looking hungover and sheepish.

"Mornin'," he offered.

"Long night?" she asked.

"I meant to come home."

"You always mean to come home."

Of her four brothers, Zane was the most prone to partying.

"Everything go okay here?" he asked.

"Mostly." She didn't want to rehash the nightmare. There was no point. "Chase got pretty cramped sleeping on the sofa."

A flash of guilt crossed Zane's face. "Why didn't he use the guest bed?"

"He did, once we figured out you must have had a better offer."

"It was a better offer. Got any coffee?"

"On the counter."

He headed for the kitchen, pausing as he passed her. "Sorry, little sister."

"You should apologize to Chase. He's the one you co-opted and then abandoned."

"Morning, Zane." Chase ambled into the living room.

His hair was damp from a shower, and he looked more relaxed than he had the middle of the night. His painkillers were obviously working.

"Sorry I left you stranded," Zane said.

Chase gave an unconcerned shrug. "No problem. I can heal up here, as well as I can in that motel room." He gave Maddy an offhanded smile. "Company's better anyway."

There was nothing intimate about the look, but her stomach fluttered anyway. Her cheeks grew warm and she worried Zane would see her reaction. She quickly turned toward the kitchen.

"You both want coffee?" she asked over her shoulder.

"Please," Chase said. "Black is fine."

Riley came running down the hall, full of exuberance and enthusiasm. "Can we ride a horse today?"

Maddy turned back to tell Riley that Chase couldn't stay any longer.

"My ribs are pretty sore," Chase said, bending down on one knee to talk to Riley.

"I'll take you riding," Zane offered.

Given what looked like a wicked headache, Maddy could only conclude Zane was feeling more guilty than usual. She appreciated his offer. Hopefully, his presence would distract Riley.

Riley frowned. "I want to go with Daddy."

"Riley, that's enough," Maddy said. "Chase is hurt, and Uncle Zane is being very generous with you."

She met her twin brother's gaze.

"Still?" Zane asked in an undertone.

Chase looked up at Zane. "I haven't been able to figure out what to say."

"You better say something," Zane said.

"I know," Chase agreed.

"It's up to me," Maddy said.

No matter how difficult, she'd have to find the words to make Riley understand. This wasn't Chase's problem, and it wasn't Zane's problem.

She sat down on the closest chair to be eye level with her son. "Riley, Chase has to leave soon. I know you've liked—"

"No!" Riley shouted.

He instantly pushed tighter against Chase, who sucked in a breath of obvious pain.

"Riley," Maddy admonished, rising to get him. "You're hurting him."

"It's okay," Chase said.

"You can't leave," Riley wailed. "You just got here."

"There's a bull ride coming up in Billings," Zane said, obviously trying to help by giving Chase an excuse to leave.

"Daddy's hurt," Riley said, with an unexpected level of perception. "He can't ride bulls if he's hurt."

"He's got you there," Chase said to Zane, a glimmer of what could have been admiration or amusement in his gray eyes.

Maddy couldn't believe he was taking this so casually.

"Hurt or not," she said. "Chase has to leave us."

Riley held on tighter.

"There's no rush," Chase said.

"We can't keep this up." She wasn't an expert in psychology, but she knew as a mother this couldn't be good for Riley.

"We won't," Chase said. "But it doesn't have to be instantaneous."

"That's not fair to you." And she was a long way from

thinking it was the best solution.

"Let me worry about me. There's not much I can do but sit around for the next couple of days."

"You're not coming to watch in Billings?" Zane asked, seeming surprised.

Whether or not a bull rider was riding, they were passionately interested in how the other competitors fared. And there were always opportunities to learn more about specific bulls and consider future techniques to use when riding them.

Before Chase could respond, Maddy's phone rang.

She reluctantly left the conversation to answer.

"Hello?"

"Maddy? It's Jessica Staples calling from the casino."

The greeting got Maddy's attention. She moved a little ways down the hall, and Chase and Zane's low voices seemed to disappear.

"Hi," she said. "Hello. It's nice to hear from you."

"I'm glad I caught you," Jessica said. "I know it's been a few weeks, but I've been reviewing your resume."

Maddy held her breath.

"One of our dealers had a family emergency. And, well, with your experience, I realize it's very short notice, but could you start tonight?"

"Tonight?" Maddy's glance went automatically through the doorway to Riley. This was nowhere near the ideal time to leave him.

"I'm afraid we need someone right away."

"Sure. Yes." Maddy would work it out.

Somehow she'd work it out. She desperately needed the money.

"It would only be temporary to start. But"—Jessica gave a light laugh—"you know how these things go."

Maddy was grateful to get her foot in the door. Jobs were scarce. She didn't have that many skills. And card dealers made good money at the local casino complex. Plus, she'd applied for late shifts, so Riley would be sleeping most of the time she was away.

"I understand," she said. "I'd be happy for the opportunity."

"Fantastic," Jessica said. "Start time is normally eight, but you'll need an hour or so to get back up to speed."

"I can be there at seven."

"We'll see you then."

Jessica signed off and Maddy hung up the phone.

She took a moment to breathe then walked back into the living room.

"Everything okay?" Chase asked, still on the floor with Riley.

She gave him a nod. "Zane?"

"Yeah?"

"Any chance you can curtail the partying tonight and take care of Riley?"

Babysitting wasn't her brother's favorite activity, and

she'd find a permanent sitter as soon as she could. But she didn't want to leave Riley with a stranger right now.

"You got a hot date or something?"

"I got a job."

Chase looked sharply up at her.

Zane's brows knit together. "What do you mean you got a job?"

"At the casino. Dealing cards."

Zane shook his head. "No, Maddy. I'm not going to let you do that."

She'd expected some pushback and she wasn't about to let his attitude rattle her. "This isn't about you *letting* me do anything."

"Riley needs you."

"It's the late shift. He'll be asleep."

"And you'll exhaust yourself."

"I'll be fine."

"I'm calling Lucas."

She took a step toward Zane, ready to stop him if he pulled out his phone. "Don't you dare."

"If it's about money."

"You know it's about money, and I'm not taking money from Lucas. I'm standing on my own two feet."

Zane's voice grew louder. "So this is about pride?"

Maddy became aware that Riley, and for that matter Chase, was hanging on their every word.

"Can you do it or not?" she asked Zane.

"Not," he said.

"Fine," she barked back, trying not to let his lack of support hurt her feelings.

"Because I can't," he said. "Skeeter and I are leaving for Billings this afternoon."

"You don't have to explain."

"Don't do that," Zane said.

"I'm not doing anything."

"You're getting that hurt little puppy dog expression on your face. I want to take care of you."

"No, you want to strong-arm Lucas into taking care of me."

When she saw his expression, she knew how much her words had hurt him.

She immediately backtracked. "I'm sorry. I didn't mean it that way."

Like all of her brothers, Zane felt acutely the loss of their family's land. After their parents had been killed, they'd struggled to keep the cattle ranch going, but they'd failed. If they'd kept it going, Maddy could have made a contribution to running it while still staying home with her son. They all knew that.

In the silence, Chase came to his feet. "I think the answer's pretty obvious."

Maddy and Zane looked at him.

"I'm not going to Billings."

She was both touched and unsettled by the offer. Riley

would obviously love for Chase to stay. But how could she take such a generous offer? And how could she let Riley continue with his fantasy?

Chase's tone went low. "I don't think you'll get an argument from Riley."

Maddy didn't know what to do. She didn't want to impose on him any more than she wanted to impose on her brother Lucas.

"It'll save me paying for a motel," Chase said.

"This isn't about today or tomorrow," Zane said. "Let me call Lucas."

"Lucas is off the table." There was no way Maddy was going to take an allowance from her oldest brother.

Her brother made good money in the New York financial sector, but that money was his. It didn't belong to the family, and it wasn't up to her or to Zane to put a call on it.

"This shouldn't be so hard to decide." Chase's voice was kind, but at the same time firm. "If you need to work, you need to work. This is the best short-term solution for Riley. I'm assuming this is all about Riley."

It was all about Riley. And it was all about her, about what kind of mother she'd be, and what kind of woman she'd be. Her husband's life insurance hadn't been enough. It hadn't been nearly enough for her to run a house and raise a son. Dealing cards at the casino might not be the perfect solution, and it didn't have to be forever. But at least she'd be able to fix the carpets and pay for preschool.

"Okay," she said to Chase. "I'll take your offer. I'd rather do that than call Lucas."

Zane heaved an exaggerated sigh, raking a hand through his dark hair. "You're going to regret this."

"She's taking a job," Chase said to Zane in a reasonable tone. "Not getting a tattoo."

"A tattoo?" Maddy wasn't following Chase's logic.

"I was trying to think of something permanent that you might regret."

"What's wrong with a tattoo?"

"Do you *have* a tattoo?"

"A vine. It's pretty and very discreet."

"Where—" he seemed to stop himself.

"I'm tagging out," Zane said, taking a few backward steps toward the door.

Chase gave her a grin. There was a twinkle in his eyes that she desperately hoped Zane would miss.

"Can you drop me at the motel?" Chase asked Zane, moving for the door himself. "I'll grab my stuff and come back with my truck."

"Are you sure about this?" she asked.

She wanted to give him one final out. Not that she knew what she'd do if he took it.

He turned back to look at her with an intensity that made her knees go weak.

"I am absolutely sure."

THE NEXT MORNING, Chase discovered how difficult it was to keep a three-year-old quiet. He was trying to let Maddy sleep in after her late shift. He'd heard her arrive home around two-thirty.

He'd thought about getting up to say hello but decided against it. He liked Maddy. He liked her a lot, and he wasn't sure he could trust himself in the wee hours of the morning not to make a pass at her.

It was clear she had a whole lot on her plate. She had to be worn out from the challenges in her life, and he had no intention of taking advantage of that.

"It's smelly," Riley said, wrinkling his nose at the adhesive patch pad Chase was tucking under the edge of a hole they'd cut in the living room carpet.

"Talk quietly," Chase said, demonstrating what he meant by saying the words in a whisper. "Mommy's sleeping."

"It's smelly," Riley repeated in a whispered voice.

"Don't touch it," Chase said, finding it easy to read Riley's intentions from his expression.

"Is it hot?" asked Riley, thankfully still keeping his voice down.

"It's sticky," Chase said. "Like honey."

"Can I taste it?"

"No." Chase made a face. "It's yucky, and it'll make you sick."

"Yuck."

"Exactly. Yuck. Now, move back just a bit."

They were kneeling on the floor. Chase picked up the carpet square cut to the right size.

"I need a little more room," Chase said.

Riley wriggled back, while Chase carefully set the carpet down.

"Help me press it down." Chase used the flat of his hand to anchor the carpet to the wet glue.

Riley happily helped, patting his small hands against the carpet. The carpet ends they'd found in the basement weren't as faded as the carpet on the floor. But, overall, the match was pretty good.

"Better," Chase said, pulling back to look.

"Better," Riley echoed.

"What are you doing?" Maddy asked, dressed in a T-shirt and her pajama bottoms, she leaned against the end of the wall.

Chase still found the outfit incredibly sexy. He realized there had to be something wrong with him, because he'd bet there weren't a lot of guys into green plaid.

"We chopped up the carpet," Riley announced with glee.

He jumped up and trotted over to Maddy, giving her a hug.

"I found a roll end in the basement," Chase said. "It's not perfect, but we got rid of a few worn spots."

"It needs to be replaced," she said, looking embarrassed.

"You can still replace it. This just buys you a bit of time."

"Thanks. And thanks for letting me sleep."

He retracted the blade, tucked the cutter into his pocket and came to his feet. "You got in pretty late."

"Still…"

Riley tugged at her hand. "I helped," he said proudly.

She scanned the carpet. "You fixed the spot by the door too," she said in obvious surprise.

"And under the window," Riley said. "And where Daddy dropped the paint can."

"You remember that?" Maddy asked Riley.

Riley nodded. Then a strange look came over his face, and he glanced at Chase.

Chase pounced on the moment.

He crouched back down so he was eye level with Riley. "Did you know that some people have more than one daddy?"

Riley's lips pursed, and his eyes squinted down.

"Sometimes, when one daddy has to go away, a different one comes into a little boy's life."

"Daddy always comes back," Riley said. But his eyes took on the sheen of tears.

"Daddiess come back when they can." An unexpected weight settled on Chase's chest as he spoke.

For some reason, he was reminded of his own father leaving. The situations were completely different. Mac Garrett hadn't died, and Chase had been fourteen when it happened.

But he'd left and he hadn't come back.

Riley swallowed. "Are you going away?"

Chase decided he'd pressed enough for now. "I'll have to go ride bulls again."

Riley gave what looked like a brave nod.

"But not today," Chase said. "Today we're going to paint your bike."

It took Riley a moment to react. When he did, he seemed guarded, as if the offer was too good to be true. "What color?"

"Any color you want," Chase said.

"Can it be red?"

"Sure."

"Like a fire engine?"

"Chase." Maddy's cautious tone had Riley glancing at her with apprehension.

Chase kept his tone light. "You have something against red?"

"Your ribs."

He waved away her concern. "It's light work. A little sanding, a little spray paint and polish."

"You don't need to do this."

"There's a hardware store in town?"

"Yes, but…"

"Can you go get your shoes?" he asked Riley.

"Yes." Riley grinned from ear to ear then took off down the hall.

"You want to come along?" Chase asked Maddy.

She looked worried, and a shot of anxiety went through him. It occurred to him that there might be something about the situation he didn't know. He might have made her life more difficult by trying to help.

"Maddy?" He moved toward her, ready to apologize and make it better.

"What I want," she said on a note of wonder, "is to thank you all over again."

"For what?" He couldn't stop himself from inching closer.

"For last night." She gestured to the carpet. "For this. And now his bike."

"It's nothing."

"But most of all," she continued as if he hadn't spoken, "for telling him he could have two dads."

"It's true." Chase had moved too close. He knew it, but he couldn't bring himself to back off.

"I saw his face," she said. "He's thinking. It's a start, a gentle start."

"It's a start," Chase agreed. He was very glad the thought had occurred to him.

She closed her eyes, and her shoulders drooped in what looked like relief.

"Hey." He couldn't help reaching out to touch her.

Then he wrapped an arm around her. It seemed like the most natural thing in the world to pull her into an embrace.

The second he did, he remembered her state of dress. She was naked under the thin T-shirt, and her loose breasts touched his chest. She felt delicate in his arms, and he was overcome with a wave of protectiveness. It was followed by an equally potent wave of desire.

His hug tightened, and she rested her head on his shoulders.

"I shouldn't do this," she whispered. But she seemed to be talking to herself as her arms went around him.

"You're not doing anything," he assured her.

"I'm leaning on you."

"It's okay."

"I feel weak. I can't be weak."

"You're not weak. You're resting. Everybody needs to rest."

"I don't know you," she said.

"You will."

"You're leaving."

"I am," he agreed. "But not yet. Not today."

She nodded against his shoulder.

He moved his head so that he could whisper in her ear. "Lean away."

"Am I hurting you?"

Her question took him by surprise. But then he remembered his ribs. He'd forgotten about them. With her in his arms, they didn't hurt at all.

"No."

"You're lying."

"I'm not. But it wouldn't matter. I can take it."

"You're a cowboy?"

"That I am, ma'am. And no self-respecting cowboy would let a little thing like broken ribs keep him from aiding a woman in distress."

She laughed at that. "I like you, cowboy."

"I like you, Maddy." He pulled back, partly because he wanted to look at her face while they spoke, and partly because Riley was going to be back any second.

Their gazes met. He smoothed back her hair then he stared at her lush lips for a long moment. After an internal battle, he settled for kissing her forehead. Even that small gesture felt absurdly erotic. He loved the taste of her skin, the scent of her hair, the feel of her slender shoulders beneath his palms.

He had to back away now. But he knew for certain that when she came home tonight, he wouldn't pretend to be asleep.

WHEN MADDY GOT home, Chase was still up. She'd known he would be, and she knew why. She'd tried all night long to forget the feel of his embrace. And she'd tried very hard to pretend she hadn't sent the signals she'd sent him.

"You're up." She pretended to be surprised as she peeled

off her high shoes. Her feet were killing her.

"How was your night?" He was sitting on the sofa, a single lamp burning in the living room.

"It was fine." She padded barefoot across her newly patched carpet, trying to quell her growing desire for him. "Like riding a bike."

"You've dealt cards before?"

"Only at charity events. I was too young to do it in the casino. But I waited tables in their restaurant during high school. So I know how the place runs."

"You look tired."

"I am tired."

"You want a drink?"

She did, but she wasn't comfortable jumping into a fling.

"There's a decent bottle of bourbon in my bag," he said when she didn't immediately answer.

"Chase." She sank down on the opposite end of the sofa, deciding she owed it to him to be honest. "I don't want to give you the wrong idea."

He sat up straighter. "And what idea is that?"

"I know." She didn't know how to say it, except to come right out and say it. "I know we kissed and earlier you hugged me. And I hugged you back. And you're a good-looking guy and all."

"What's the idea you don't want me to get?" he prompted-ed.

"You're a bull rider. You're here for a week, maybe two

at the outside. I've got a son, and I'm not about to fall into bed with you just because—"

"Just because you want to?" There was a twinkle of amusement in his eyes.

"Just because *you* want to," she corrected. He might have guessed at her attraction to him, but she was equally aware of his attraction to her.

His voice was low, deep and melodic. "Who says I want to fall into bed with you?"

"You stayed up and waited for me."

"I didn't have expectations." His words said one thing, but his expression said another.

"But you had hopes."

"I'm a man. And you're amazing. And I absolutely had hopes. I still have hopes."

"Chase."

He gave his head a shake. "I'm not that shallow. I also stayed up because I wanted to have a conversation. I wanted to see how it went for you at work. I thought you might like to know how things went here with Riley."

She experienced a flash of worry. "Is everything okay?"

"Riley's fine. I gave him a bath, read him a book, and he went to sleep."

"You gave him a bath?" She didn't know why that touched her so much.

"He was pretty dirty from playing outside."

She leaned back, feeling herself relax. "He always gets

dirty."

"He's a boy."

"He certainly is." Her son might be confused about Chase at the moment. But besides that, he was an ordinary, healthy happy young boy.

"And how are *you?*" Chase looked like he genuinely wanted the answer.

"My feet are killing me."

He grinned and held out his broad hand. "Give 'em here."

She wasn't about to fall into that trap. "Chase."

"You think this is seduction 101?"

"Yes."

"It's not. It's sympathy 101. Nothing happens tonight that you don't want to happen. I swear to that."

She knew his words were meant to comfort her. Unfortunately, they didn't. Because she was more worried about herself than she was about Chase. Everything he'd said and done in the past few days told her he was a principled gentleman.

She, on the other hand, seemed to want to throw herself into the arms of a handsome bull rider who was only passing through town. She'd always questioned the morals of the women who did that. Maybe she'd been too judgmental.

"You need me to save you from yourself?" he guessed with frightening insight.

"I do not," she lied.

"Then there's absolutely no danger here." He leaned down and lifted one of her feet, setting it on his knee and pressing his thumb into her heel.

She knew she should stop him, but she wasn't strong enough to say no. His circular strokes were heavenly. For a few minutes she sat silently and selfishly, letting him massage his way along her foot.

"Where did you lean to do that?" she asked.

"Internet how-to video."

The answer made her smile. "Seriously?"

"I read that pregnant women appreciated foot massages."

"Pregnant women?"

A funny expression crossed his face. "I want to have children someday."

"Are you married?" She tried to pull her foot away, but he stopped her, holding it fast.

"I'm not married. I'm not engaged. And I don't have a girlfriend."

"Are you sure?"

He gave her a lazy smile, and resumed massaging. "I've been with myself my whole life. I think I would have noticed."

She accepted the answer, relieved and glad he was unattached.

"What about you?" he asked softly into the quiet.

She found the question odd. "My husband died."

"Since him? Before him?"

"Before him, I was in high school. I was a tomboy back then. I wasn't dating anyone."

"You must have had offers. You're a knockout now, and I can't imagine you've changed that much in four years."

"You're exaggerating. Besides, I had Zane and three older brothers. There weren't a lot of guys getting past those guard dogs."

"But Chase Barrett did."

"They liked him." Her mind went back to their first date and Lucas's reaction. "He reminded them of themselves, and they thought he'd take care of me."

There was an edge to Chase's tone. "Instead he got you pregnant."

"We didn't tell anybody, and we got married right away."

"Your brothers aren't stupid," Chase said. "They knew."

"Then they preferred to pretend it hadn't happened." She didn't want to talk about this anymore.

Chase seemed to catch her change in mood. He stopped asking questions and leaned down to lift her other foot, silently massaging it. The first few strokes were blissful, and she closed her eyes, leaning her head against the sofa.

He pressed circles into her heel, then longer strokes along her arch. His hands were large and strong, releasing tension from the balls of her feet.

"Did you love him?" Chase asked, his voice resonating deep.

Maddy blinked herself back to reality. "What?"

"Did you love him?" Chase repeated. "You had to marry him."

"I didn't have to marry him."

"At the very least, the decision was complicated by Riley."

She stared at him. "What is it you want to hear, Chase?"

His hands stilled as he gazed back.

"Nothing," he finally said. "I'm sorry. It's none of my business."

She pulled her foot away, sitting up straighter and curling both feet beneath her.

"I'm sorry," he repeated.

"It's okay." She wasn't mad.

There was no reason for her to be mad. Chase was the one doing her so many favors. And he kept doing them.

"How are you feeling? Your ribs?"

"Getting better." He shifted his body, his expression tightening as he moved. "Slowly but surely."

"You're still really sore," she guessed.

"I'll be sore for a while. Sore's not a problem."

"You should stop doing so much work around here."

"I'm not doing much."

"Well, that's about the biggest lie I've ever heard."

"I painted a bike. It was fun, not work."

"And you fixed my carpet. And when the sun comes up tomorrow, am I going to find something else? Like maybe you painted the porch or replaced the roof?"

"The porch does need painting," he said.

She picked up a throw pillow and tossed it at him. It hit him in the chest.

"Ouch."

She immediately regretted her action. "I'm so sorry."

He grinned. "I'm joking. Even in my wounded condition, it'll take more than a pillow fight to lay me out."

"You're hopeless."

"What color?"

"What color what?"

"What color do you want your porch?"

She came up on her knees and shook her head. "Oh, no you don't."

"I don't see how you're going to stop me."

"I'm… Well…" She searched her brain for an idea.

Truth was she didn't see how she could stop him either. And if she was being completely honest, she wasn't sure she wanted to stop him. An image of him sweaty and shirtless with a paintbrush in his hand came up in her mind.

It was staggeringly sexy, as was Chase.

"I've got you stumped," he said.

He had her more than stumped. He had her confounded and disconcerted. Her feelings for him were a jumble of gratitude, admiration, and desire.

She wanted him. It was going to take a lot of self-control to stay out of his bed.

Chapter Five

CHASE WAS FEELING better every day. He'd given up the painkillers, and he could feel his strength returning as he ran the sander along the floor of the porch, removing the chipped white paint.

Maddy had complained at first, but he could sense that her heart was never in it. She felt guilty for taking his help, that much was clear. But he could also tell she appreciated the few things he was able to do around her house. She'd made it clear she was on a budget, and it was obvious her husband hadn't done a lot of maintenance between his bull-riding events.

She didn't have a shift at the casino today and she was pitching in, scraping the decorative rails. Riley was riding his newly red bike around the concrete patch in front of the garage, making siren noises.

Chase caught a movement in the corner of his eye and looked up to see a car pulling up the driveway. He shut off the sander.

"You've got company," he said to Maddy.

She looked up and came to her feet.

"Know who it is?" he asked.

"I don't recognize the car."

It was a dark blue, late model sedan, clean and shiny compared to a lot of the vehicles he'd seen around town.

It came to a halt, and Chase could see a man was driving.

"It's my brother," Maddy said, setting down the scraper and brushing her hands across the fronts of her jeans.

"Zane?" Chase asked. He couldn't see very well, but it didn't look like Zane. The man was wearing a blazer or a suit jacket.

"Lucas." Maddy rubbed her hands across her cheeks then she smoothed her hair.

"Which one is he?" Chase couldn't help going on alert.

If he remembered correctly, Lucas was the brother from New York City. The one Zane had threatened to call in over Maddy getting a job.

"New York," Maddy said. "He's the oldest."

The car door opened and Lucas stepped out. He was dressed in a business suit, wore a pair of wingtips, and he looked to be impeccably groomed.

Chase refused to feel self-conscious about his own appearance. He was working with his hands, not attending a board meeting.

"What's he doing here?" Chase mused out loud.

She shot him a look of frustration. "Do I look like I know?"

"Do you think Zane called him?"

"He better not have." She started down the stairs to meet her brother.

Chase's instinct was to go with her, but he hung back. The man was her brother. There was nothing for Chase to contribute to the conversation.

The two hugged, even though Maddy's clothes were marred by sawdust.

After that, the body language went downhill.

Lucas was frowning. Maddy was shaking her head. It was clear there was frustration in their exchange of words. When Maddy pointed at Chase, and Lucas shot a glare his way, Chase decided it was time to make a move.

He set down the sander and stripped off his safety goggles, making his way down the stairs and along the path to the driveway. He stopped a few feet short of the pair.

"Chase," Maddy said, "this is my brother, Lucas."

"Pleasure to meet you," Chase said, holding out his hand.

Lucas shook. His grip was firm, his hand callused. He might be dressed like a banker, but it showed that he'd grown up on the ranch.

"Maddy tells me you've been babysitting."

Chase could hear both a challenge and the mockery in his voice.

"That's right," Chase answered easily. "Riley needed care."

"He's done a whole lot more than babysit." Maddy rose

to his defense. "He saved Riley's life. He's doing endless work around here."

"I thought you were injured?" Lucas addressed Chase.

"You spoke to Zane."

"I told him not to call you," Maddy said.

Lucas returned his attention to her. "He didn't. Zane talked to Eli. Eli called me."

"Eli needs to mind his own business," Maddy said.

"You are our business, little sister." Lucas looked to Chase again, obviously sizing him up. "Everything about you is our business."

Chase couldn't help but smile at the subtle challenge.

"Something funny?" Lucas asked.

"Stop," Maddy ordered her brother.

"I'm only painting her porch," Chase said.

He had nothing to hide here. He might be attracted to Maddy, but he hadn't made a single serious move on her. He was respecting her wishes, and his conscience was clear.

"Out of the goodness of your heart?" Lucas drawled.

"Uncle Lucas!" Riley came scampering across the uneven lawn, making a beeline for Lucas.

Lucas readily scooped the boy up in his arms. "You're getting so big, Riley."

"I am," Riley happily agreed. He pointed. "My bike is red."

Lucas dutifully looked to the bike. "I see that. It looks good."

"We painted it. I got to pick the color."

The look Lucas gave Chase said he was onto him. It wasn't the time to set Lucas straight. But Chase got the sense he'd have that opportunity before Lucas left.

"I hear you started a job," Lucas said to Maddy, letting Riley slide to the ground.

Riley headed back toward his bike.

"Please tell me you didn't fly all the way from New York to tell me I'm wrong to start working," Maddy said.

"You're wrong to start working."

"I need to earn a living, Lucas. That's what I told Zane, and it's still true."

"If it's about money…"

"It's about more than money."

Lucas glared at Chase. "Do you need to be here for this?"

"No," Chase admitted. He didn't.

Maddy's tone went sharp. "Don't chase him away."

"I want to talk to you in private."

"Bullying me alone isn't going to work any better."

Chase folded his arms across his chest. Lucas might be her brother, but Chase wasn't going to stand by and let Maddy be bullied by Lucas or anybody else.

Lucas didn't say a word, but it was obvious he caught Chase's change in stance.

To Maddy, Lucas said, "You don't need money, and *he* doesn't need to be here."

"Wrong and wrong," Maddy said. "Piper has offered to

watch Riley, but she can't start until next week."

Lucas stilled, his expression going on alert. "Piper?"

"You obviously remember Piper Beauregard."

"She left town years ago."

Chase tried to guess what was going on in Lucas's mind. Something was obviously wrong. For some reason, he didn't trust Piper. But Maddy had mentioned that the Beauregards lived in the valley for decades. What would there be not to trust?

"She's back," Maddy said. "She owns the print shop now."

Lucas seemed to catalogue the information. Then he neutralized his expression. "How much money do you need?"

"Stop," she said.

"How much?"

Chase couldn't stay quiet any longer. "What have you got against her working?"

Lucas gave him a look that clearly questioned his intellect. "She has a son to take care of."

"Plenty of women work and raise children." Chase knew it was rare for single mothers to have the luxury of spending all day with their children.

"Maddy's not plenty of women."

"You do know she's over twenty-one."

Lucas's expression turned steely. "What is *that* supposed to mean?" It was obvious the turn of phrase made him even more suspicious of Chase's intentions towards Maddy.

Chase squared his shoulders. "Are you actually questioning your sister's virtue?"

"I'm questioning *your* motivation."

"My virtue is none of your business, Lucas," Maddy said.

"He said it," Lucas pointed out. "Not me."

"I haven't touched her," Chase said.

Maddy's eyes went wide in obvious astonishment.

"That's what's really got you bothered, isn't it?" Chase asked Lucas. "Well, let me put your mind to rest."

"What's got me bothered," Lucas said, articulating each word, "is that my sister is leaving my nephew with a babysitter while she flirts for tips in a casino."

"She's a card dealer, not a cocktail waitress." Chase had seen her uniform.

It was a plain black dress with red piping. Her shoulders were bare, and it was figure hugging and, sure, he thought it was sexy. But he'd find her sexy in a potato sack. He wasn't an accurate benchmark.

"I can speak for myself," Maddy said an edge to her tone. "I'm not *flirting* with anyone. And Piper will take good care of Riley. He'll be asleep most of the time I'm at work."

"And what about you?" Lucas asked. "You're going to exhaust yourself."

"I'll manage," she said.

"You don't have to *manage*."

"I'm not taking your money. It's yours. I know you're

saving."

"I'll save a little longer."

It was obvious Lucas was saving for something specific. It was just as obvious that it was none of Chase's business. A week from now, he'd move on to Missoula, or maybe he'd hold out for Tacoma. But either way, Maddy and Riley's lives would carry on without his input.

Lucas, on the other hand, would be a part of her life forever.

Chase felt a sudden shift in his perspective. What would he do in Lucas's shoes? What if he had a sister who was a single mother and needed financial support?

He'd try to ram it down her throat every bit as hard as Lucas was trying to ram it down Maddy's. And he'd be right. Because he'd never let a sister of his exhaust herself working in a casino if he had the power to stop it.

"You should listen to your brother," Chase said.

Two astonished gazes swung his way. Lucas's turned quickly to appreciation, while Maddy's turned equally quickly to anger.

Chase spoke to Maddy. "You don't have a really good argument against taking his help."

"What about independence and self-sufficiency?"

"What about Riley's well-being?"

Her blue eyes cooled in the heat of the afternoon. "Don't you *dare* try to tell me what's best for my son."

"An exhausted mother is not best for anyone."

Maddy glared at Chase then she turned on Lucas. "Neither of you can stop me from making my own decision. You might as well give up now." She turned on her heel and marched toward the house.

They watched her go.

Lucas was the first to speak. "You better not be sleeping with her."

"I'm not sleeping with her."

Lucas's look was piercing. "Then why are you still here?"

"Zane didn't tell you?"

"I talked to Eli not Zane."

Chase knew there were four brothers. He didn't know where the communication chain broke down, but it had broken down somewhere. "Then they didn't tell you."

"Tell me what?" There was more than a thread of steel in Lucas's voice.

There was no point in sugar coating it. "Riley thinks I'm his father."

Lucas's jaw dropped open.

"Yeah." Chase had an inkling of how Lucas felt. "We're trying to bring him back to reality, but we're afraid to do anything drastic."

"How can he think…"

"Apparently, I look like him and sound like him. I have the same first name, and Riley saw me bull riding." Chase could feel his throat thicken over the words and he swallowed the emotion down. "Poor little guy is desperate for me to be his daddy."

AS SHE MADE her way through the motions of the evening, Maddy felt completely alone. It wasn't that she was arguing with Lucas. She argued with her brothers all the time.

It was being at odds with Chase that had her upset. Since the moment he'd come into her life, he'd done nothing but back her moves. Through some extraordinary ups and downs, he'd had her back at every turn. And now he was siding with Lucas.

She made them all burgers for dinner. Then she gave Riley a bath and put him into his pajamas. She stayed out of sight in his room while he said good night to Chase and Lucas, grateful that he scampered back down the hallway on his own and she didn't have to go get him.

She lingered over his stories, reading to him long after he'd fallen asleep. Finally, she couldn't put it off any longer. She dreaded sitting down to talk to the two men without the buffer of Riley making everyone hold their tongues.

She had her own bottle of bourbon in the cupboard, and she stopped in the kitchen to pour herself a glass, taking a big sip before making her way into the living room.

There, Chase and Lucas seemed deep in conversation. She could only imagine plotting how to attack her together.

"He asleep?" Chase asked.

"Yes." She took another sip.

Chase's glance went briefly to the glass, but he didn't make a comment.

"Chase told me," Lucas said.

"Told you what?"

"About Riley."

It took Maddy a moment to realize what Lucas meant. He was talking about Riley thinking Chase was his father. She sank down in an armchair, giving herself a moment to breathe.

How had that circumstance not been her first thought? In such a short time, she'd grown used to Riley calling Chase Daddy. It had jarred her at first. And then she still noticed it. But lately, it had become something of a backdrop. That couldn't be good.

"Yes," she said to her brother, "it's a big problem."

"What's your plan?" Lucas asked.

"To introduce the idea slowly," she said. "Chase already introduced the concept of a child having more than one father, that sometimes fathers had to go away."

As she spoke, she realized that conversation had taken place days ago. Neither she nor Chase had done anything since, at least nothing that she knew about. And she had a hard time believing Chase would have made progress and not mentioned it to her.

"Chase isn't going to be Riley's new father," Lucas said.

Anxiety cramped her stomach. "I know that."

"He's leaving."

She couldn't stop herself from glancing at Chase. "I know he's leaving."

Was that what they'd been out here talking about? Chase's plan to leave?

"You need a long-term plan," Lucas said.

"I know all this." She wished Chase would say something. She could use his support along about now.

"Then why haven't you done anything about it?"

"Who says I haven't? When Chase leaves." She paused to take a drink, buying herself a moment and bracing herself with the liquor. "When Chase leaves, if Riley doesn't already understand, I'll make him understand."

"I'll help," Chase said.

"Riley's going to need your support," Lucas said to Maddy.

"He'll *have* my support. Don't you question my parenting capabilities."

"He'll need you here," Lucas said.

"And we're right back to it." She swallowed the remainder of the bourbon and rose to get some more.

"I'll get that," Chase said, standing up quickly and taking hold of the glass in her hand.

"Do you really think you need another?" Lucas asked.

"Back off," she said.

"I'll get you another," Chase said firmly. "Sit down."

She didn't like that it sounded like an order. She didn't

let go of the glass.

"Please," Chase said, "listen to your brother. Try not to let your emotions get in the way. He only wants what's best for you and Riley."

"Seriously, Chase. My emotions?"

"You know what I mean."

"You mean I'm a woman, and therefore I don't have it in me to be logical."

"I didn't say that."

"You might as well have." She snapped the glass from him and turned for the kitchen.

When she got there, she realized he was on her heels.

"What's wrong with you?" he asked.

"I'm thirsty." She poured herself another drink.

"Nobody's going to make you do anything you don't want to do."

She laughed at that. "You're giving a damn good imitation."

Chase lowered his voice. "Talk to him, Maddy."

"Why are you on his side?"

"I'm on your side," Chase said.

She suddenly realized how close they were standing together. His voice was vibrating through her. He smelled like sawdust and the outdoors. She wanted to touch him. She wanted him to hold her, to pull her close, and tell her everything was going to be alright. She had a wild, momentary fantasy of them taking this on together.

"Listen to what he has to say, then do whatever you want to do."

"What?" She'd lost her train of thought for a moment.

Chase took her drink. He downed it. Then he kissed her soundly.

She would have protested, but she was too surprised. Plus, she didn't want to protest. She wanted to beg him to kiss her again.

He set down the glass. "Instead of getting drunk. Talk to your big brother. This might be hard for you to understand, but the same way you want to protect Riley, Lucas wants to protect you."

"I'm his sister, not his daughter. It's not the same thing."

"He told me he was twenty-five when your father died. You were fifteen. You have to forgive him if he sometimes mixes up his roles."

"You're ganging up on me," she said.

"We are. But in the end, you're the one who gets to decide."

For some reason, his words made her feel better.

"You kissed me," she said.

His gaze went to her lips. "I did. I promised myself I wouldn't do that again." Then he turned abruptly to one side to give her room to pass. "Let's go."

It took her a moment to move. She wanted him to kiss her again. And she wanted him to want that too. But he didn't make a move.

She left the kitchen, returning to her brother.

Lucas stood.

"I need to think about this," she told him.

His gaze flicked behind her, obviously to Chase.

"But you will think about it," Lucas said.

"I will." She couldn't imagine changing her mind. But she didn't feel like arguing anymore. "Are you going back to New York?"

"Maybe tomorrow."

"Are you staying here tonight?" She couldn't see putting Chase on the sofa. But she supposed Lucas could take her bed, and she could sleep out here.

"I've got a hotel room in town."

"I can stay in a motel," Chase said.

"No need," Lucas said. "I've already checked in."

Maddy couldn't help but be surprised that Lucas would leave her here alone with Chase, given his earlier accusations. He must be convinced Chase was on his team now. Maybe that made a difference in his mind.

"I'm coming back tomorrow," Lucas said.

"I know." The thought made her tired.

He pulled her into a goodbye hug. "I love you, Button."

"I know you do." She did, even though it could occasionally be claustrophobic.

"You have options," he said as he released her from the hug.

"Do I?"

"Don't be melodramatic. See you in the morning, Chase."

"G'night," Chase said.

As the front door closed behind Lucas she couldn't seem to stop herself from speaking. "He trusts you alone with me."

"I know," Chase said from behind her.

She heaved a huge sigh. "Score one for the brotherhood." And now, she really was going to have a second drink.

"What does that mean?" Chase asked.

She ignored him and started for the kitchen.

He caught her by the arm. "Hey."

"Hey, what?"

"Hey, what's with the brotherhood comment? I told you, I'm on your side."

"Maybe," she said without looking at him.

"There's no maybe about it." He put a finger under her chin and tilted her face toward him. "I'm on your side, Maddy. I want what's best for you."

His touch was like a bolt of lightning, sending desire coursing through her, electrifying her skin, and making every hair stand on end. Her skin was reaching out for him, desperate for his touch.

Her arousal combined with her disappointment to override common sense. "What's best for me, maybe"—she blurted out—"but you don't seem to want me."

His gaze instantly darkened to pewter. "*What* did you say?"

"Lucas left us here alone."

"And?" Chase demanded.

"Clearly, he's figured out you're a Boy Scout." Once she got started, she couldn't seem to stop herself. "You fix my carpet. You paint my porch. You take care of Riley. All without making another move on me. I don't need that, Chase. I don't need another brother."

Their gazes locked together.

His voice turned to a rasp. "Are you serious?"

"Yes."

"You couldn't be any more wrong."

She hoped she was wrong. She wanted to be wrong. She was baiting him, and was fully ready for wherever it led.

The intensity ramped up in his gaze. "You're *all* I think about, Maddy, your eyes, your lips, your laugh, the glow of your hair." He reached out and rubbed her hair between his fingertips. "I go to sleep thinking about you at night, and I wake up to your image in the morning."

He stepped closer then, his thighs brushing hers, and she thought she might actually swoon. "When you wander around in the morning, I want to tear those pajamas in half. I never knew green plaid could be so sexy. But it's sexy on you. Everything's sexy on you. You want to know how I feel? What I want to do?"

Her stomach went hollow with wanting. "Yes," she managed to rasp.

"I want to kiss you until you can't see straight, until your legs give way beneath you. And then I want to scoop you into my arms and carry you to bed, strip off your clothes and make sweet, endless love to you all night long."

She swallowed. Her lips began to tingle with anticipation. Blood rushed to her breasts, peaking her nipples, while the rest of her flooded with moisture.

He brushed the back of his hand across her cheek. Then he pushed his spread fingers into her hair. "You want me to do that, Maddy? Some of it? Any of it? You say the word, and we'll do whatever you want."

"Yes," she hissed. She wanted it all, and she wanted it right now.

He touched his forehead to hers, his breath coming in uneven rasps. "Please be specific. I don't want to mess this up."

"All of it," she said. "Make love to me, Chase."

CHASE SKIPPED AHEAD to the part where he lifted Maddy into his arms and carried her to the bedroom. He hoped she didn't mind, because he didn't have it in him to wait a second longer.

He lowered her to her feet next to the bed then cradled her face, savoring the anticipation as he leaned to kiss her properly for the first time in days. Her mouth was hot, her lips soft, her scent surrounded him and he drew her fully into his arms, holding her slender body against his.

Their kiss went on and on, until he forced himself to draw back. He needed to feel her skin on his, so he stripped off his shirt, reaching for hers.

"Oh, Chase." There was worry in her tone.

It took him a moment to realize she was staring at the bruises on his ribs. They were ugly, but they were fading.

"How did you carry me?" she asked.

"Endorphins," he said. "You have me so completely turned on I can't feel anything else. Plus, you barely weigh a thing."

She reached out, her fingertips gently and tentatively stroking the mottled purple marks.

Her hands were cool and the touch felt good; it was soothing. But it also ramped up his arousal.

"Does it hurt?" she asked.

"Not right now." He started on the bottom button of her shirt.

"I don't want you to make it worse."

He parted her shirt, revealing a white lacy bra. "The only thing getting worse is how bad I want you." He pushed the shirt from her shoulders.

She smiled at him. "If you're sure."

"I've never been more sure of anything in my life."

"Okay." She leaned forward and kissed the bruise. Then she kissed him again, moving higher on his chest, over his pecs, across his flat nipples.

For a moment, he forgot everything else. His head tipped back to savor her kisses. She stroked her palms along his sides, around his back. Then she reached for his belt, popping the buckle.

"You're getting ahead of me," he muttered.

"Catch up," she said.

He released the clasp of her bra, letting it fall away to reveal her rounded breasts in the moonlight. Her nipples were dark, puckered, and pointed his way.

"You're so incredibly beautiful," he whispered, recapturing her face and kissing her deeply on the mouth.

Her tongue tangled with his and he was transported to absolute paradise. His hand closed over her breast, loving the heat, the texture, the softness. He wanted so badly to taste her.

Passion rushed through him, urgent and acute. He needed her naked. He needed both of them naked so he could wrap himself around her and never let go.

He stripped off her jeans then he pulled off his own. Moments later, they were tumbling down on the bed. He eased her beneath him, kissing her mouth, her neck, drawing her breasts into his mouth and teasing them to a harder nub. The taste was beyond his imagination.

She groaned. Her back arched toward him. Her hands gripped his shoulders, moving lower and lower along his back, until she was pressing him into the vee of her thighs.

He stroked her belly, dipping down. Her legs twitched

further apart, and he ran his fingers freely over her satin skin, drinking in her soft groans, loving how her head moved back and forth on his pillow, her hair splayed in all directions, her eyes closed, her dark lips slightly parted.

He kissed those swollen lips, drawing the bottom one into his mouth.

"Please," she whispered, stiffening under his caresses.

"Now?" He wanted to be sure.

"Right now."

He didn't need another invitation. He flexed his hips and slipped inside, feeling the moist heat of her engulf him.

He groaned, then he stilled for a moment, getting his bearings.

She moved, and he moved, and the rhythm of their lovemaking took over his brain. She was the sweetest, most beautiful woman he'd ever met. They fit perfectly together. He would breathe her essence forever if she'd let him.

He climbed higher and then higher still. Music pulsed through him, colored lights built behind his eyes. Passion tightened his body, turning his muscles to steel, and still it got better.

She gasped breathlessly and her fingernails dug into his back.

She frantically kissed his mouth, opening to him, and his tongue captured hers once more. His senses were bombarded, rushing headlong to overload.

"Oh, Chase!" Her body stiffened, then it convulsed, and

he was surrounded by the sweet heat of her reaction.

He careened over the cliff alongside her, his own body pulsing with ecstasy. The waves went on and on, until he collapsed on top of her, pinning her against the soft mattress.

Their labored breaths synchronized. The world came back into focus.

"Am I hurting you?" He moved to roll off her.

But her arms tightened around him. "Don't move."

"You're okay?"

"I'm better than okay. Just... stay... exactly... as... you... are."

He smiled at the rapture on her face. "You bet."

After a minute, she opened her eyes.

He gazed into their depths, thinking all over again that she was the most beautiful woman in the world.

"That was..." She was still breathless.

He waited, but she didn't finish the sentence.

"I don't have the words either." He smoothed her hair from her face. "Except to say that you're amazing. You're beyond amazing."

She smiled. "You're not so bad yourself. Even if you are hampered by an injury."

"Imagine what I could do at full strength." He wasn't feeling a scrap of pain at the moment.

"I don't know if I could handle that."

"You don't?"

It was on the tip of his tongue to make a joke. But anything he said would allude to him sticking around until he got better. That wasn't something either of them should touch in a moment like this.

Instead, he said, "Lucky for you, you got the restrained version."

Her smile broadened. "You're such a liar."

"You saw the bruise."

"You can't possibly do it any better than that."

His ego absorbed her words. "I'll take that as a compliment."

"You should."

He gave her a tender kiss. He didn't want to joke anymore. "While we're dishing out compliments, you blew me away."

She sobered. "It's been… a while."

"I know." He shifted to his side and cradled her against him, spooning her back into his stomach, wrapping his arms around her to keep her warm.

"There are things you don't know about me," she said softly.

"There are things that I do." He kissed the curve of her neck.

"Like why I fought so hard against Lucas."

"You don't owe me an explanation."

Chase was the one who should apologize. He didn't know why he'd stepped in to the middle of that. He'd been trying to help. But he didn't want to fight with Maddy. He didn't want to fight with her about anything.

"This house," she said. Then she seemed to gather her thoughts. "I'm already a big drain on the family. I don't want it to get any bigger."

It was clear she wanted to talk. And he wanted whatever she wanted.

"How so?" he asked.

She glanced around the dim room. "After my parents died, and we discovered how much my father had borrowed against the ranch, Lucas, Eli, and Wyatt worked like dogs to try to keep the land in the family. Zane and I were only fifteen, but he pitched in too. I didn't realize how bad things were. I was busy flitting my way through the drama of high school. And then one day, Lucas told me we'd lost it. Beef prices were down, and we couldn't make our payments, and all we had left were five acres and this house."

He pressed his lips to the top of her head. "I'm sorry you had to go through that, all of that."

Chase had lost his father as a teenager. But his mother had been around for another decade. And their ranch was never in jeopardy.

"So now," she continued, "today, the five of us own the house. I'm living here for free while my brothers try to earn enough money to buy our land back."

"Zane seems pretty footloose." Chase couldn't recommend bull riding as a way to get rich quick.

"Don't let him fool you. He's won a lot of money over

the past few years. He's coming up fast in the standings. And he always works when he's not riding."

Chase wouldn't have guessed that.

"Eli's a good horse trainer. He found a job on a big race horse spread in Oregon. And Wyatt's flying as a bush pilot. It's a camp job, so he has no expenses, and he saves every penny he makes."

"You have to take care of Riley." Chase didn't think she had any cause for guilt.

Maddy nodded against Chase's shoulder. "I know. Maybe I can't contribute at the moment, but I'm not going to take away their money. This house is our only asset. If it wasn't for me, they could sell it and add to the pot. But they can't, because of me, and I hate it."

Chase wrapped her more solidly in his embrace. "I wish I could help."

As he uttered the words, an idea floated into Chase's brain. It was as compelling as it was far-fetched.

She raised his hand to her lips and gave him a kiss. "You're helping me with Riley. I can't tell you how much that means to me."

It meant something to Chase too. Riley was coming to mean something to Chase, not to mention how he felt about Maddy.

He realized that from the moment he'd met her, those frantic minutes at the bull ride, all the way up to now, he'd been planning to eventually leave her life, to walk out, move on, and never be part of her life.

But what if he didn't?

What if he stepped in to help her?

What if he somehow kept them connected instead of letting her become a fond memory?

Chapter Six

WHEN CHASE ANNOUNCED he was going into Dead-wood, Riley immediately begged to go along. Maddy hadn't wanted to saddle Chase with babysitting duty, but when he'd insisted he didn't mind, she'd agreed. Truth was, she was grateful for a little time alone.

She was still working through the fact that she'd made love with Chase last night. She didn't regret it for a minute. But that didn't mean she knew how she felt about him.

He was sexy, that went without saying. She liked him. Evidently, she liked him an awful lot. But he was still temporary, moving on with the AEBR circuit as soon as he was healed. And Riley complicated matters. Her son was still convinced Chase was his daddy. She had to address that, and she had to do it soon. She couldn't keep putting it off in the hope it would resolve itself.

She heard a vehicle in the driveway, and couldn't stop a surge of disappointment. It would be Lucas coming back to pressure her about money. She would have liked a bit more time alone before she had to argue with him again.

She opened up the front door, surprised to see Piper

coming up the walk.

"Is this a bad time?" Piper called out.

"It's fine," Maddy said. She definitely preferred Piper's company to Lucas's. "Coffee's on."

"Good," Piper said, making it to the porch.

She took a look around at the partially sanded porch. "I see you've been working."

"I had some help."

"Nice."

"Come on in." Maddy held the door wide.

"Thanks. I needed to get away from home for a while and talk to someone who's not in the throes of a teenage hormone breakdown."

"Tristan again?"

"Turns out, I'm the worst mother in the world."

"Forget the coffee," Maddy said. "I've got a bottle of Chablis in the fridge."

"It is afternoon," Piper said, the lilt in her voice telling Maddy she was definitely up for some wine.

Maddy led the way to the kitchen, taking the wine from the fridge and finding two stemmed glasses in the top cupboard. "Tell me what happened this time."

Piper's fifteen-year-old son, Tristan, seemed to be quickly becoming a handful for his single mother.

"He wants to go camping with his friends."

"Unchaperoned, I take it."

"I quote, 'Jeremy's brother is almost seventeen.'"

Maddy poured the wine. "And Jeremy's brother will be in charge?"

"He'll be the driver. And I'm assuming the guy with a line on the bootlegger."

"You think they'll drink?"

Piper accepted a glass of wine and raised it in a toast. "If it was just Tristan and Jeremy, probably not. But it's an older crowd, at a bush party to boot. Those two would be in way over their heads."

The two women sat down at the table.

"You'll have to stick to your guns," Maddy said.

"I'm definitely going to stick to my guns. But first, I need a drink." Piper waved the glass. "Just so you know, I do get the irony."

"We're both over twenty-one."

Piper took a swallow. "Thank goodness for that."

Maddy smiled, thinking of the longer-term future with Riley. "Sometimes I wonder what I've gotten myself into."

"Single motherhood is not for the faint of heart. But you've got the golden years ahead of you. It lasts until they're about thirteen. Then, watch out. Where is Riley, by the way?"

"He's in town. With a friend who's been staying at the house."

"Who is she?"

"It's a he."

Piper raised a curious brow.

"It's not like that." Maddy ignored the fact that it had been exactly like that last night. "He rides with Zane on the circuit. He got hurt at the Deadwood ride, and he's staying here while he's healing up." Maddy found she was reluctant to share the details of Riley's delusion any further than the family.

"You do not want to get mixed up with a bull rider." Then Piper seemed to realize what she'd said, and her expression was immediately filled with regret. "I'm sorry."

"It's okay. Not all bull riders are the same."

"Not all bull riders are your husband." Piper reached out to touch Maddy's hand. "How are you holding up?"

Maddy thought back to Chase and the night before. It was the first time ever that she'd slept with anyone besides her husband. She should probably feel guilty. But she didn't.

Making love with Chase had felt good. It had felt right. She didn't regret it for a moment.

"One day at a time," she said to Piper. "I think getting a job is the right move."

"It'll bring balance. It'll also bring a paycheck. Money becomes more and more important, especially when kids learn to read designer labels."

"How are things going at the print shop?"

Piper had put up her small nest egg to buy the business in order to bring Tristan to Deadwood. She'd confided in Maddy that she'd worried about the crowd he'd started running with in Chicago.

"It's holding its own. There's a lot of competition from online firms, but I'm trying to cultivate some distant customers on the design side. I'm not making a fortune, but I'm paying the rent."

"It'd be nice not to worry about money."

Since she'd been pregnant right out of high school, Maddy hadn't had the chance to go to college. Once Riley was in school, she promised herself she'd look into some distance classes. There must be some way to better prepare herself for the job market. She couldn't see being a card dealer for the rest of her life.

She heard another car in the driveway. This time, it was definitely going to be Lucas.

"Here we go," she muttered, downing the rest of her wine.

"What's up?" Piper asked.

"That'll be Lucas."

Piper's face paled a shade. "Lucas is here?"

"He flew into Deadwood to harass me."

Piper suddenly looked worried, almost frightened. "I didn't know he was in town."

"What's wrong?"

"Nothing."

"Piper?"

"Last time I saw him, we had a huge fight."

"That was years ago."

Lucas and Piper had graduated high school together. As

far as Maddy knew, they hadn't seen each other since Piper left for college.

"He won't have forgotten."

"What—" Maddy stopped herself.

The fight was none of her business. Besides, Lucas was going to walk in any second. Even if Piper wanted to tell Maddy, there wasn't time.

The front door opened and his footsteps sounded.

Piper's fingers tightened on her wineglass.

"Maddy, I've got about an hour—" Lucas stopped in his tracks. He stared at Piper as if he'd seen a ghost.

"Lucas," Maddy said. "I'm sure you remember Piper."

The two watched each other, and the silence stretched. Maddy couldn't help but wonder what on earth had happened between them that the hard feelings had lasted this long.

She stepped into the awkward silence. "I told you Piper was going to help me out with Riley."

"Piper," Lucas said in a tense voice.

"Hello, Lucas."

Piper rose shakily to her feet. "I'll get out of your way."

"You don't need to rush off," Maddy felt compelled to offer.

Although, judging by the expression on Piper's face, there was no way she was sticking around.

"I'll call you later," Piper said to Maddy.

"Sure. Anytime."

Piper seemed to hesitate before walking past Lucas, as if she was afraid he might reach out and grab her.

Lucas seemed to sense her hesitation. He moved to one side, and she walked past, through the living room and out the front door.

"What on earth was *that*?" Maddy asked her brother.

"What?" Lucas asked.

"You and Piper. You acted like enemy combatants."

"No, we didn't."

"Yes, *you did*."

"I didn't notice. It was nothing."

"Lucas."

He walked to the table and pulled out a chair. "We don't even know each other anymore. I'm here to talk about you."

"I haven't changed my mind."

He heaved a sigh as he sat down.

"You want some wine?" she asked.

He reached for Piper's abandoned glass. "No sense letting this go to waste."

"I don't want to fight with you, Lucas."

"And I don't want to fight with you."

"You need your money," she told him in no uncertain terms.

"I'm making a lot of it."

"And you have plans for it."

"My plans," Lucas said, "are to take care of my family. You're my family. Riley is my family. The best way for me to spend some of it—and I'm only talking about *some* of it—is on the two of you right now."

"And I'm telling you, we don't need it. What's more, I won't take it. I'll keep my job and tear up your checks."

Lucas downed the wine. "You are the most stubborn woman in the world."

"And *you* are too accustomed to being in charge."

"I'm obviously not in charge here." His gaze drifted to the doorway where Piper had left.

"Is there any way you're going to tell me what's going on between the two of you?" Maddy asked.

"There's nothing to tell."

"You know I'm going to ask her next time I see her."

His gaze shot back to Maddy, piercing. "Don't."

Maddy twirled her empty glass, savoring the small victory. "You don't want me to ask her about *nothing*?"

"Mind your own business."

Maddy was happy to keep the conversation off her and Riley. "Did the two of you bury a body together?"

Lucas clamped his jaw.

A wave of anxiety washed through Maddy. "You're kinda scaring me here."

"There was no body. It was nothing. We were kids. She was stupid, and I was a jerk. We're both more embarrassed than anything."

The front door swung open.

"Mommy, Mommy," came Riley's excited voice, "come

see what we bought."

CHASE HAD MIXED emotions at seeing Lucas's rental car in the driveway. If his plan was going to work, the two men had to have a serious conversation. But any conversation between them was going to be more complicated today.

The last time he'd spoken to Lucas, Chase had sworn he hadn't slept with Maddy. Now he had, and he was willing to bet Lucas would flip if he found out. It would have been nice to have a bit more time to work up to it.

Riley was in the kitchen, turning a circle to show Maddy his little Stetson and his new six shooter belt.

"It goes bang," he told her, pulling out the cap gun.

"Not in the house," Chase cautioned, joining them from the doorway.

Maddy and Lucas were at the table and it looked like they were drinking wine.

Chase checked his watch. It was only two in the afternoon. He hoped they didn't need the alcohol for any specific reason—like Lucas was about to take Chase's head off.

"You bought him a gun?" Maddy asked.

Chase couldn't read her expression, so he decided to take the question at face value. "You have something against guns?"

"I have something against loud noises."

Chase relaxed just a little. "I told him to use it outside."

There was resignation in her tone when she answered. "And I'm sure he'll remember that every time."

Riley was already cocking the hammer.

"Riley," Chase warned, giving him a censorious look.

"Yes, sir." Riley let his gun hand drop and dipped his chin. "Only outside."

"Did you have some lunch?" Maddy asked Riley.

"I had a hotdog and French fries. Bang! Bang!"

"We went to the Orange Bow Café," Chase said.

"You're spoiling him."

"I didn't want him to starve."

"And the present?"

"Is it my fault the hardware store has a toy section? You can't take a kid in there and come away completely empty-handed."

Chase's objective had been twofold. Sure, he wanted to make Riley happy. But he also wanted Riley to forget about their visit to the lawyer's office. As he'd hoped, the cap gun and the hotdog were far more interesting than Chase's conversation with the lawyer.

"Mommy, can I play on the porch?" Riley asked.

"I'll watch him," Chase offered. To Lucas, he asked, "Join me?" He held up the six-pack he'd brought back from town.

Since Lucas hadn't called Chase out, Chase was going to assume Maddy had kept the change in their relationship

CHASE

private.

"Sounds good," Lucas said easily, rising from his chair.

Maddy looked relieved to be left alone. Chase could only surmise Lucas had already made another pitch about giving her an allowance.

The two men crossed the front porch and settled in two faded wood Adirondack chairs on the lawn.

"The two of you have a big problem," Lucas said as he opened the bottle of beer.

Chase tensed, waiting for the hammer to fall. Maybe Maddy had shared more confidences with her older brother than Chase had guessed.

But Lucas pointed to Riley. "He's your biggest fan."

"He's a great kid," Chase said, relieved.

"But he's not your kid."

For some reason, the words offended Chase. They were true, and Lucas was only stating a fact. But it rankled none the less.

"I have a proposal for you," Chase said, letting the statement slide.

Lucas angled his body, looking curious.

"It's about the house."

"What house?"

"This house. Your house."

"You mean Maddy's house."

"She told me it belonged to all of you."

"It does." Lucas's tone was implacable. "But she lives

135

here. No if, ands, or buts."

"We're in agreement on that," Chase said.

"Why, thank you." Lucas's sarcasm was clear.

Again, Chase blew past the possible negative turn in the conversation.

"I have some money," he said. "I recently sold some land and the capital is just sitting there."

"And?" Lucas was looking decidedly suspicious.

"My proposal is that I buy this place from you. Maddy keeps living here as long as she wants, and she takes her share of the profits to use for expenses."

Lucas's eyes narrowed. "You swore you weren't sleeping with her."

Chase looked him in the eyes. "Everything I said to you yesterday was true. But Maddy's a terrific woman. Riley is a great kid. They haven't been dealt the easiest hand in the world, and I want to help."

Lucas was clearly suspicious. "What's in it for you?"

"An investment, for one. I fully expect this place to appreciate. And my dad walked out on me when I was a kid. My mom had to raise me alone. I know it's not an easy thing to do."

Chase moved his attention back to the view and took a drink of his beer. He wasn't lying, but he wasn't fully disclosing either.

"We don't need your help." Pride colored Lucas's tone.

"You don't," Chase agreed. "But Maddy does. Because

she's not going to take your money, and you can't force her to quit her job."

Lucas tapped his index finger against his beer bottle.

"I know you're trying to buy back your family's spread," Chase said. "You can use the money towards that."

"This is part of my family's spread. What's to stop you from selling it out from under us?"

"That's not my plan," Chase said. "But write anything you want into the sales contract. You can have right of first refusal. Or I'll agree not to sell until Riley's eighteen. Or both. Whatever you want."

"She lives rent free."

Chase shot Lucas a look of disbelief. "That would be the whole point, wouldn't it?"

"I don't trust you," Lucas said. "I don't know you, and I don't trust you."

"Then we'll put it in the fine print."

"There's something you're not telling me."

There was definitely something Chase wasn't telling him. But that thing had happened after he made his pledge yesterday, and he wasn't about to give Lucas an update.

"Think it over," Chase said, turning his attention to Riley and pretending the answer didn't matter. "There are plenty of other real estate deals in the world."

Lucas went silent, while Riley plunked away with his cap gun.

Chase sipped his way through is beer, letting his mind

wander to Maddy. She was back in the house right now. He pictured her puttering in the kitchen, maybe picking up toys in Riley's bedroom. In his imagination, there was a glow to her face, and she hummed as she worked.

Then he pictured her in her pajamas. And then she was naked, hair tousled, lips swollen, and she was whispering his name.

"It's not just my name on the title," Lucas said, interrupting Chase's thoughts.

"Maddy's?" Chase guessed, bringing himself back to reality.

"And my brothers."

"So you're considering my offer."

"I'm considering it." Lucas paused, then seemed to make up his mind. "If you can bring Maddy around, I'll get my brothers on board."

"Done," Chase said.

"I'm having my lawyer go over the fine print."

"If he prefers, he can draw up the whole contract himself," Chase said, finished with this part of the conversation. Coming up with a deal they could both agree on was going to be a piece of cake.

Right now, he was framing up his pitch to Maddy.

Moments later, his brain switched from that to what he'd do with her after Lucas left, and then to what he'd do after Riley went to sleep.

He couldn't wait to hold her in his arms again.

He decided the details about the house could wait until tomorrow.

"NO," MADDY SAID the next day as she stood up from the kitchen table, taking a dinner plate in each hand.

Chase watched her ramrod straight back and knew he had a bigger challenge than he'd anticipated on his hands. "What do you mean no?"

"It's not a complicated word, Chase." She dumped the plates into the sink.

"You haven't even heard me out."

"I don't have to hear you out to give you an answer." She returned for a second load, picking up the butter plate and the basket of home baked rolls.

"Stop clearing the table," he said.

"Why?" She frowned at him. "Are you still hungry?"

"I'm not still hungry. I'm trying to have a conversation with you."

She turned her back and marched across the kitchen. "The conversation is over."

He came to his feet. "Why is it over?"

"If I start explaining why, then it's not over, is it?"

Riley ran past the doorway, making a motor noise and carrying a toy airplane, and Chase came to his feet and began helping her clear the table.

"You're not making sense." He snagged the salt and pepper shakers in one hand and an empty platter in the other.

"I'm making perfect sense. You're the one who's lost his mind."

"It solves both your money problems," Chase said, replacing the salt and pepper shakers on the shelf above the stove.

"I don't have two problems."

He set down the platter and counted to three before responding. "I meant both your money problem and Lucas's money problem."

"I don't have a money problem," she said airily. "I have my money problems solved."

"By working at the casino?"

"Exactly."

"Maddy." He set his hands on her shoulders and urged her to face him. "It's a good investment. I'm making a good investment."

She turned. Her cheeks were flushed, her voice low-pitched. "It's a pity purchase, Chase."

"This isn't pity. I have the money just sitting there."

"And it's *your* money." Her glare was aimed at his chin. "This is even worse than Lucas."

"This isn't me helping you." He hesitated, but then spoke the truth. "This is me helping Riley."

Her gaze suddenly darkened like a prairie storm. "He is *not* your son."

Chase felt like she'd slapped him. He dropped his hands and took a step back. "I know that."

"Do you, Chase?" There was a quaver in her voice. "Do you? I notice you haven't told him that yet."

"And neither have you!" The second he spoke them Chase wished he could bite back the words.

"Daddy?" Riley's voice was hesitant in the kitchen doorway.

Chase felt the world sway beneath him.

"You're right." Maddy tipped up her chin and square her shoulders. "Not telling him was a mistake. And I'm going to fix that right now."

"No," Chase pleaded with her.

She marched toward Riley.

Chase was instantly on her heels. "Maddy don't. Not like this. Not when you're angry."

"Riley, sweetheart." She took his hand.

"Yes, Mommy?" There was both worry and confusion in his little voice.

"Can you come and sit down with me?"

"Maddy, please." Chase searched for the words that would stop her from taking such a rash action.

"Mommy needs to tell you something."

Chase knew he shouldn't follow. He knew he should give her some space. But he couldn't bring himself to back off. A rock had formed in the pit of his stomach, causing an ache of dread.

"I'm flying my plane." Riley broke away, and spun, making loud engine noises.

"*Riley*," Maddy admonished.

Riley stopped spinning. He wobbled. Then he sat down hard on the floor.

The fight seemed to go out of Maddy and she sank down beside him.

"Riley, honey." She gathered him close.

"Maddy, don't," Chase told her softly.

She didn't look up. "Remember how I told you Daddy had died? That he was in heaven?"

Riley looked at Chase in confusion.

"This Chase isn't your daddy," Maddy said. A single tear trickled down her cheek. "Your daddy's dead, and he isn't coming back."

Riley looked up at her. "He's dead?"

"Yes. I'm so sorry, baby. But he died."

Riley looked at Chase again, his little eyes narrowing, his brain obviously working hard to comprehend what he was hearing.

Chase couldn't for the life of him think of anything to say that would help.

Riley struggled out of Maddy's arms.

She reached for him, but she didn't seem to have any strength left.

He padded his way to Chase, seeming to search Chase's face for answers.

Chase crouched down to meet him, and Riley immediately clambered onto his bent knee. Chase couldn't bring himself to push Riley away, so he stilled and balanced him on his thigh.

"Daddy?" Riley said. He took a gulp of air and swallowed.

Even though Maddy's expression pleaded with him to back her up, Chase couldn't bring himself to tell Riley it was all true. Chase wasn't his daddy.

"Daddy," Riley whispered, resting his little cheek against Chase's chest. It seemed like an eternity ticked by. "Are you getting a divorce?"

The words stunned Chase. His brain scrambled for a response.

"It's not a divorce." The hard lump in his stomach moved to his chest, and he held Maddy's pained gaze as he spoke. "This is different."

"Bobby's daddy got a divorce." Riley's arms clung tighter and tighter to Chase. "And his mommy says he's dead to her now."

Maddy gave an audible sob. Her shoulders slumped, and she raised a trembling hand to her lips.

"This is different," Chase repeated. "I was never—" He swallowed. He tried again. "I was never—" He couldn't do it.

Silent tears ran down Riley's cheeks.

"I'm sorry," Chase mouthed to Maddy.

She shook her head. She clenched her hands together. Her voice was hoarse when she spoke. "What have we done?"

Chase didn't have an answer for her.

In his mind, he went back over the night they'd met. Should they have said something the minute it happened? Or was there a point along the way where he should have spoken up, made Riley understand? Should he have at least tried?

He didn't know. He couldn't think.

For now, all he could do was hold Riley's little form and pray there was a way to make him see reality without completely devastating him.

While the sun slowly sank behind the mountains, Chase mentally questioned all his choices up to this minute. The tears slowly dried on Maddy's cheeks, and Riley's breathing evened out as he fell asleep.

Chase broke the long silence. "He needs you."

Maddy gave a nod. Her face was pale, and her eyes were hollow.

"I don't need the money," Chase said. "It's just sitting there in the bank."

"Chase."

"No." He wasn't going to let her refuse. "I sold a place in Lethbridge. It was big. It was beautiful, and I'd planned to spend the rest of my life on that land. It didn't work out."

That was all he'd planned to say. But Maddy didn't respond. She just watched him with those gentle, beautiful eyes that made him want to spill all of his secrets.

"I was going back to live in Twin River," he told her. "My family has land there, and I was getting married, and we were going to have a family."

Maddy's eyes now went wide with surprise.

"But my fiancée—my *ex* fiancée—had other plans. Funny thing." He could almost bring himself to laugh, almost but not quite. "She'd had other plans for a while. I just didn't know about them. I sold the land in Lethbridge for her. She was the one who wanted to live in Twin River Valley, close to her family, close to her friends. So, once we broke it off…"

He stopped, not wanting to go any further down that painful path. He wondered if he'd made his point. Was it enough for Maddy to agree to let him buy her house?

"What happened?" she asked.

"I sold the land," he repeated.

"Why did you break up with her?"

Chase had no desire to look like a fool. But he didn't want to keep secrets from Maddy either.

"She slept with my best friend."

"Oh, Chase."

This time he did manage a chopped, cold laugh. "The baby was his."

"She was pregnant?"

"I thought it was mine. I had this whole happily-ever-after thing built up in my mind. I came home that night to surprise her, to tell her I'd sold the land. And he was there, and they were together, and that's when they told me I wasn't the daddy."

He found himself looking down at Riley. "So you can see. I don't care about the money. The money is nothing."

"I'm so sorry, Chase." There was deep sympathy in her tone.

"I don't want your pity." He wanted her respect, but tonight wasn't the time he'd be getting it. "Let me buy the house. Stay home with Riley. Help him get through this."

She shook her head. Then she nodded. Then she pushed her hair back from her forehead.

"Okay," she said.

"Okay?" His heart lifted.

"Okay, I'll take Lucas's money."

Chase stilled. "You'll what?"

"You're right." Her gaze went to Riley, and there it softened. "I need to be with my son."

"Weren't you listening? I can buy the house."

"Lucas is my brother."

"So what? I'm your—" Chase stopped himself. What was he going to say? Her lover? Her friend? Riley's fake father?

"You were Lucas's backup plan," she said.

Disappointment washed through Chase.

But she was right. He wasn't a part of her family. He couldn't even be called a friend. He was just a guy, a stranger passing through who happened to look like her dead husband.

He forced himself to accept her decision. Then he forced himself to speak. "Do you want me to leave? Would it be easier if I left?"

It took her a long time to answer. "Maybe not tonight."

The knot in Chase's chest slacked off ever so slightly. "I think it would kill me to leave it like this."

"I don't know what to do, Chase." Her eyes turned glassy with tears.

"We'll figure it out." He promised.

He'd never wanted to hold her more. He wanted to sweep her into his arms, cradle her tight, and soothe her fears. And then he wanted to carry her off to bed, make sweet, healing love to her all night long.

But he couldn't do that. He was a bastard for even thinking of it. She was mentally and emotionally exhausted. The last thing she needed was Chase's lust.

He rose slowly to his feet, supporting Riley's head on his shoulder. "I'll put him to bed."

"I'll help."

Together, they made their way down the hall.

Maddy pulled back the covers and Chase laid Riley down on the sheets, placing his head on the little pillow. She turned on the nightlight, while he pulled off Riley's shoes.

"I'll clean up the kitchen," he told her, tucking the covers around Riley's shoulders. If he concentrated on Riley, he wouldn't give in and pull Maddy into his arms. "Go take a hot bath. Have a drink. Get some sleep."

"Thank you," she whispered.

He straightened, wishing with all his heart that he deserved her gratitude. "I'm so sorry."

"It's not your fault. It's nobody's fault." Her shoulders drooped. "It just is."

But nothing just "was." Everything was the result of choices. And selfish choices had adverse consequences.

He'd been selfish to stay this long. He could pretend it was all for Riley, but that would be a lie. Chase had also stayed because of Maddy. He'd fallen hard for Maddy. But it was clear that what she needed right now was support from her family, not from him.

Maybe not tonight, but it was time for him to go. It was past time for him to go.

Chapter Seven

FOR SEVERAL DAYS now, Maddy had been climbing the walls. She missed Chase, and she hated that she missed Chase. Riley remained convinced Chase was coming back soon, and every day he begged to go to the next AEBR event in Missoula to watch the riders.

Maddy had told him Chase wouldn't be at the event, but Riley wasn't deterred. It was clear bull riding made him feel closer to his father. She didn't know if that was a good thing or a bad thing. She wanted him to remember his real father. She didn't want him to keep mixing the two men up.

Then Piper offered to go with her to Missoula. It was the weekend of the teenage campout, and the trip would keep the sullen Tristan out of town while his friend partied. Maddy was desperate enough to agree. And Tristan had a learners' permit, so offering to let him do part of the driving was just enough of a carrot to overshadow the campout.

Maddy had double-checked the roster to confirm Chase wasn't riding. He'd said he planned to spend some time in Wyoming before rejoining the tour, so she decided it was safe to go watch Zane.

Early Thursday morning, they'd piled in Piper's minivan for the nine-hour drive. On the way, they'd stopped in Billings for dinner. By the time they hit Bozeman, Tristan was worn out from driving. And by the time they hit Butte, both Riley and Tristan were sound asleep in the back seats.

"Quietest I've seen him in months," Piper said from behind the wheel. "Well, except for Saturday and Sunday mornings. I swear a bomb could go off and he wouldn't wake up."

"I remember sleeping like that as a teenager," Maddy said. "Well, up until I got pregnant. Morning sickness is no fun."

"Is that why you and Chase got married?" Piper asked. "Tell me if it's none of my business."

"That's okay," Maddy said, focusing on the line of headlights passing the other way. "It wasn't a real secret. My brothers never said anything at the time, but a baby that comes two months early doesn't weigh eight pounds."

"I guess not."

"Funny, though. We never ever did talk about it. I hadn't realized that until Chase pointed it out."

"After Riley was born?"

"Last week."

"What?"

Maddy became momentarily flustered. How could it be that her default Chase was now Chase Garrett?

"Maddy?"

"It was Chase Garrett who said something."

"The Chase who just stayed with you?"

"I told him we hadn't told my brothers that I was pregnant before the wedding. And he said they weren't stupid. They knew. And he's right. They had to have figured it out."

Piper gave her an odd look. "You and Chase Garrett discussed your marriage? You getting pregnant with Riley?"

"We did. Does that seem weird?"

"It seems interesting."

Maddy had said a lot of things to Chase Garrett, things she never would have imagined saying to a stranger, never mind a bull rider. But Chase hadn't stayed a stranger for long. They'd been thrown together under the most personal of circumstances. Perhaps it was inevitable their relationship would become intimate.

"So, did you sleep with him?" Piper asked with studied casualness as she gazed out the windshield.

"Well, that was blunt," Maddy said.

"And *that* wasn't a no."

Maddy glanced into the backseat to make sure Tristan was sleeping soundly.

She lowered her voice. "If I did, would that be bad?"

"I hope not."

Maddy wasn't sure how to take Piper's answer.

"I'm guessing," Piper continued, "that Chase was the first guy you slept with after Chase died. That was confusing, but you know what I mean. So I hope it was good. I hope it was very good."

"He was," Maddy said. "And it was."

"I'm glad." Piper glanced at her. "You don't feel guilty, do you?"

"I don't. Maybe I should. But… well… Chase, my husband Chase, wasn't… exactly…"

"That good in bed?"

"What?" Maddy couldn't hide her shock. "No. That wasn't what I was going to say at all. I mean, he wasn't great. He was fine." She was getting more flustered by the second.

"Fine?"

"Okay. I'm going to say this. I'm just going to say it."

Piper waited.

"I'm not sure I was his first choice as a lover."

"Did he *tell* you that?" Piper sounded aghast.

"No. He didn't. But I know he slept with other women. On the road. At events. I saw some text messages, and when I confronted him, he didn't deny it."

"Oh, Maddy."

Maddy slouched down in her seat. "He had to marry me. He never said it that way, but looking back, I know he would have been intimidated by Lucas, Eli, Wyatt, and Zane. In the circumstances, the smartest thing he could do was pretend to love me."

"I'm sure he loved you."

"I'm not."

Maddy had never said it out loud. She'd feared it more

and more for the past couple of years. But she'd never admitted it to anyone.

"Are you okay?" Piper asked.

"Yes. I'm fine. Thanks for listening."

"Of *course*. I'm happy to listen. I'm happy to do anything that helps."

"It feels odd to admit it. And I do miss him, for my sake as well as Riley's. But sometimes I don't know how to act. I'm grieving, but not in the way most young wives would grieve."

"There's no set way to grieve. And all marriages have their problems. Scratch that. All lives have their problems." Piper glanced in the rearview mirror at their sons.

"Riley thinks Chase Garrett is his father," Maddy blurted out.

"What?" Piper swerved the minivan and quickly corrected. "What did you say?"

Maddy gave Piper the story in a nutshell. "Since the direct approach was an abject failure, I'm going to keep dropping breadcrumbs. I think I'll have to wait for him to figure it out for himself."

"He will," Piper said with conviction.

"Eventually." Maddy agreed with that. "But it's so hard to watch. We miss Chase Garrett so much."

"We?"

Maddy nodded, tired of holding it inside. "I miss him, Piper. He was pretty wonderful. He was great with Riley. He fixed things up around the house. He held me. I haven't been held like that in… well, ever, I think. He's got this big strong hug, and when I put my head on his shoulder, I could swear nothing is ever going to hurt me again."

There was a smile in Piper's tone. "I don't need to ask if he was a good lover. He was a great lover."

"He was a great lover."

"I had that once," Piper said. "It was so long ago, I can barely remember it. And it didn't last."

"Tristan's dad?" Maddy asked, knowing Piper had been pregnant while she was in college.

"Tristan's dad."

"What happened to him? Did you ever consider getting married?"

"No. It was a fling. He went to a different school." Piper flipped on the signal to take the coming exit ramp. "He doesn't know," she said softly.

Maddy wasn't sure she heard right. She glanced back at Tristan again. He was stirring with the deceleration of the van.

She leaned close to Piper. "He doesn't know?"

"He never will," Piper whispered in return.

"Are we there?" Tristan asked from the backseat.

"Not yet," Piper said louder. "We're stopping for fuel."

"You okay?" Maddy asked Piper in an undertone.

"It's been a long, long time. And I'm better than okay."

Maddy couldn't help but admire Piper's upbeat attitude.

It had obviously been years since she'd seen Tristan's father. And it was clear from her tone that she'd missed him.

Maddy tried to picture years without seeing Chase. She tried to picture years without experiencing the strength of his embrace. It left her feeling hollow and bleak.

She hadn't even made it a week, and she missed it all so very badly.

MISSOULA HAD SEEMED like a natural meeting point when Lucas asked Chase to meet with him and his three brothers. Lucas told him that Zane was riding at the AEBR event, Eli was working just one state over, and Wyatt had been able to make a stopover on a cargo flight to Wyoming. Lucas, it seemed, could set his own schedule and had the resources to travel anywhere he wanted.

Chase had said goodbye to Riley a few days earlier, letting him think he was going to a bull-riding event—which he'd known then would eventually be true. His plan was to gradually pull away from Riley, maybe stop by in a month or so, just for the day, just to keep in touch. It would be hard on both of them, but he couldn't see any other path forward right now.

Maddy had already told Lucas she'd take his money. But the brothers wanted to meet with Chase anyway. Chase was curious. He wondered if Lucas might not have all the cash flow he needed to follow through with his offer to Maddy. Chase supposed he'd find out soon.

He walked into a bar and grill off Main Street in downtown Missoula to meet the four Merrick men. It was a clean place, working class, with lots of wood, practical tables, and a gleaming bar that stretched around the center of the room.

Lucas was there with Zane and the other two. All were tall, fit, with dark hair and what looked like trademark blue eyes. Lucas was urbane in a suit. Zane was scruffy in dusty jeans and plaid shirt. Chase guessed Wyatt was the one with neatly trimmed hair, wearing cargo pants and a khaki green T-shirt. While the brawniest of the four had to be Eli, unshaven in rust-colored, double-front work pants.

Lucas introduced Eli and Wyatt, confirming Chase's guess, and Chase took a seat.

"Do they know the whole story?" Chase asked Lucas.

Eli sat up straight, his shoulders square. "We know you offered to buy the house, that Riley thinks you're his daddy, and that you didn't sleep with our sister. Are we missing anything?"

"I was referring to the house," Chase said.

He didn't have any intention of delving into his relationship with Maddy. He supposed he wasn't surprised they'd discussed the situation with Riley.

"We don't like guys messing with our sister," Eli said, gaze narrowing on Chase.

The comment seemed to come out of left field and

Chase didn't know how to react.

"We didn't much like what the other Chase did," Eli continued.

The vehemence in his tone caught Chase off guard. Was this some kind of an intervention? Had they appointed themselves the family vigilantes?

"Good thing I'm not him," Chase said evenly, tensing, waiting to see where the conversation would go.

"Good thing," Eli said.

"This isn't what we're here to do," Lucas told Eli, tone firm. He switched his attention to Chase. "We have a proposition for you."

"You want me to buy the house?" Chase guessed.

Lucas looked surprised by the statement. "She already agreed to let me help."

"I know." Chase glanced around at the four men. "I thought maybe you needed the extra cash."

Zane spoke up. "Speaking of cash, exactly how much money do you have to invest?"

Chase turned to Zane. "I can afford the house."

"Well, we have a different proposition for you," Zane said.

"I told you I'm not sure about this," Eli said.

"Let Zane talk," Wyatt said.

Chase waited, curious for Zane to elaborate.

"You've met Rory Douglas." Zane referred to the oldest bull rider on the circuit.

"Sure," Chase said.

Rory was a gregarious guy. Jokingly called Gramps, he had advice for all the young cowboys. And his advice was good.

"Rory has a place for sale in Montana. Well, it might be for sale. There's story behind it. But—"

"But"—Lucas stepped in, talking overtop of his younger brother—"our story is that we can't get the Merrick land back. We looked hard for a loophole in the original lien, but it wasn't there. The new owner has title, fair and square, and he's not selling. Even if we were willing to pay above market value, he won't budge."

"We're not going to be held hostage," Eli said.

"So, back to Rory," Zane said. "His spread is for sale below market value."

Eli pushed back in his chair with a huff. "And there's a good reason for that."

"It has a bad history," Wyatt said.

"And this has to do with me how?" Chase asked.

He was following the conversation just fine. Trouble was, it hadn't yet made any sense.

"We thought you might be interested in the real estate investment," Lucas said.

"In your house," Chase said again. He assumed they meant to use the proceeds from the sale of the house to help buy the Rory Douglas spread.

"In the Douglas Ranch," Lucas said.

"You want me to buy a ranch?" Chase already had a ranch he wasn't using. He couldn't see buying another.

"As an investment," Lucas said. "You wouldn't run the ranch. We would. You'd be our partner."

Chase paused. He looked around at the four men, gauging their expressions, wrapping his head around the unexpected offer.

Wyatt flagged the waitress. "Can we get another pitcher of draft?"

Noting the other men were all halfway through their beer, Chase filled the empty glass in front of him so the waitress could remove their pitcher.

"Back to my original question," Zane said. "How much do you have to invest?"

Chase took a drink then set his glass back down in front of him. "Enough."

Lucas smiled.

Eli scowled.

All Chase could think of was Maddy. If he went into partnership with her brothers, he'd be sticking around on a permanent basis. The confusion with Riley wouldn't last. And he'd miss having the kid call him Daddy. But he could still be in their lives.

He'd take it. Whatever that looked like, he'd take it.

"We have two million," Lucas said. "The bank's good for fifty percent. We need two million more."

"You have to tell him the whole story," Eli said.

BARBARA DUNLOP

"The Douglas Ranch, Marietta Montana," Chase said. "I know part of the story. I doubt anyone knows the *whole* story."

"He's thinking about it," Wyatt said to his brothers.

"I'm thinking about it," Chase agreed.

He was way past thinking about it. If there was a dotted line, he'd be signing on it right now. He wasn't put off by the tragic past of the Douglas land. They could build a new house. It wasn't the land's fault that a terrible crime had been committed there.

"You have the two million?" Zane asked.

"Does Maddy know about this?" Chase asked.

"You have a problem with our sister?" Eli asked.

The question struck Chase as absurd. How could anyone have a problem with Maddy? Maddy was wonderful.

"Stop it," Lucas said to Eli.

"There's something going on there," Eli said.

"He's not Chase Barrett," Lucas said.

"I thought you all liked Chase Barrett," Chase couldn't help but asked them.

"She was eighteen," Eli spat.

"Yeah." Chase found something he could agree on with the combative Eli. "I can't say I was impressed when I found that out."

"They did get married," Wyatt noted.

Eli was glaring at Chase again.

"Somebody want to tell him I'm the good guy?" Chase

160

asked no one in particular.

He was trying to keep it light, but he sure hoped this didn't turn into any pointed questions about his relationship with Maddy. He wasn't going to volunteer information, but he wasn't going to lie to them either. And if they knew the whole truth, he suspected things were going to get more than interesting.

"Can we talk about the ranch?" Wyatt asked.

Chase was coming to like Wyatt. "I want to talk about the ranch."

"You have the two million?" Zane confirmed.

"I have the two million," Chase answered.

"And you're driving a twelve-year-old pickup?"

Chase chuckled. "Still works fine. I didn't sell my spread to spend the money."

"Why did you sell it?" Wyatt asked.

Chase considered how to answer the question. "Didn't need it anymore."

"There's something going on with this guy," Eli said.

"I sold it for a women," Chase said. "Then it didn't work out between us. Do you want my investment or not?"

"We do," Lucas said, sending a glare Eli's way. "We'll have to go look at the land. But Rory's got plenty of pictures, and it looks really good so far. Our thought was that Eli will manage it. The operation will service the debt, and we'll split any profits."

"And if there's a loss?" Chase asked.

He wasn't particularly worried about a loss. He'd take a loss if it kept him close to Maddy.

"You don't think I can run a ranch?" Eli asked.

"It's a logical question," Lucas said. "I'd be worried if he didn't ask."

"I don't know you," Chase said to Eli. "We'll need operating capital for at least the first year," he said to the rest of them. "Probably more like three."

"I can provide ongoing capital," Lucas said.

"Wyatt and I will kick in what we have," Zane said. "And I'll work on the ranch between AEBR events."

"Assuming the deal checks out, I'll match whatever operating capital you put in," Chase said to Lucas.

"Exactly how much money do you have?" Zane asked, a lilt of humor to his voice.

"Enough," Chase said again, smiling back.

He was beginning to like Maddy's brothers. Even Eli might grow on him over time. Chase was inclined to give Eli some slack. He was clearly the pit bull of the family, and he had no reason yet to trust Chase.

Eli was protective of Maddy. Chase could respect that. He was even glad about it. Maddy and Riley needed a few champions in their corner.

MADDY SWIPED THE motel room key across the scanner in

the open air walkway on the second floor. Riley was standing by her side, Piper and Tristan had just carried their bags into their own room next door.

"Daddy!" Riley cried out. In an instant he was off down the passageway.

Maddy's stomach lurched with worry. "Riley, come back." But as the words left her lips, she saw Chase at a room three doors down.

He lifted his gaze to meet hers, and a pressure wave seemed to race down the breezeway toward her, nearly knocking her back on her heels.

Chase was here. He was in Missoula. He was supposed to be stopping in Wyoming.

Riley launched himself into Chase's arms, and Chase scooped him up, giving her son a hug.

"Are you ridin', Daddy? Are you ridin'?"

"The doctor says I have to wait."

Riley pouted. "Awww."

Maddy set down her bags, drawn toward him.

He watched her progress.

"Hey," he said when she got there.

"You're here."

"I am."

"What happened to Wyoming?"

Chase got a curious look in his eyes. "Have you talked to Lucas?"

"Lucas? What's Lucas got to do with anything?"

Riley frowned and batted Chase's chest. "But you said you were gonna ride bulls again, Daddy."

"Not this weekend," Chase said. "Maybe next weekend in Tacoma."

"I'm comin' to Tacoma," Riley announced.

Chase gave Riley his full attention. "Buckaroo, you remember what I said about some little boys have two daddies?"

"No," Riley said, gazing down at the floor.

"Sure, you do."

"Chase." Maddy gave her head a small shake. "Not tonight."

"You sure?" It was clear Chase was trying to do the right thing.

"It doesn't have to be tonight."

Chase gave a nod.

Piper's voice sounded behind Maddy. "What's going on out here?" Her footfalls echoed on the painted concrete walkway.

Maddy turned, putting on a smile as she struggled to come to terms with Chase's presence. Obviously he was here to watch his friends and competitors. It made sense. And she was glad to see him. She didn't want to be glad, but she was.

"Piper," she said, "this is Chase Garrett."

The interest in Piper's expression amped up, making Maddy nervous about what she might say. "It's very nice to meet you, Chase."

"Mom?" Tristan's voice was slightly whiney from the motel room. "I'm hungry."

"Hello, Piper," Chase said, offering his hand.

"Mom?" Tristan appeared on the breezeway.

"You'll survive," Piper called over her shoulder.

"Are you coming to the party tonight?" Piper asked Chase.

Maddy had mentioned that it was traditional for sponsors, bull riders, and their families to attend an opening party. With Zane on the circuit, they'd be welcome to attend.

"I hadn't thought about it." Chase looked to Maddy. "You?"

"Too late for this one," she answered, reaching to take Riley from Chase.

But Riley clung tight.

"You must be getting sleepy, buckaroo," Chase said.

"No," Riley answered mulishly.

"It's getting pretty late."

"Tristan could babysit," Piper offered.

"Me?" Tristan asked in obvious consternation as he arrived beside them. "I don't wanna be stuck—"

"It's nearly your bedtime too," Piper said in a warning voice.

"That's bogus," Tristen complained.

"It'd be a paying gig," Chase offered.

"Chase, no," Piper said.

Maddy stepped in. "I don't want to impose on Tristan."

She completely understood that a fifteen-year-old boy would hate to babysit while everyone else went out to a party. Especially since he'd imagine all of his friends having a wild and exciting time back home.

"How much?" Tristan asked Chase.

"Tristan!" Piper admonished.

"It's a fair question," Chase responded. "He's doing a job for us. He should be paid fairly." Chase reached into his pocket and extracted a few bills. "I'll even spring for pizza." He handed the bills to Tristan, who looked down at them.

"Nice," said Tristan, a smile growing on his face.

"How about this?" Chase said to Riley. "I'll tuck you in while your mom gets ready. Then Tristan can stay with you for a while."

"Okay, Daddy."

Chase looked to Maddy. "Is that okay with Mommy?"

"Like Mommy has a choice." Maddy knew she had been completely boxed in.

"Mommy will like the party," Chase said with a satisfied smile.

"I know Piper will like the party," Piper said.

Maddy shook her head, pretending to be annoyed. But she would like the party. Chase was going to be at the party, and she'd missed him a lot. They'd agreed it made sense for him to leave. But right now she wondered why. Why was being apart from him better than being with him?

"Let's get you settled," Chase said to Riley as he started towards their room.

This time, Maddy was able to make the key work.

While Chase helped Riley into his pajamas, and Tristan called for pizza, Maddy used the bathroom to change into a pair of skinny jeans and a butter yellow blouse. She pulled on a pair of tan, high-heeled ankle boots to jazz up the outfit. Then she brushed out her hair and applied some makeup.

It felt like she was going on a date. It wasn't a date, of course. But she had butterflies in her stomach all the same. She couldn't help picturing a dance with Chase. She wanted to do even more than dance, but with Piper along and Zane most certainly attending the party, they were going to have to be circumspect.

When she exited the bathroom, Chase looked up. His gaze took a tour from her hair to her boots, and he gave her an appreciative smile.

"Looks like you're ready to go."

"My mom'll take an hour," Tristan said, not bothering to look up from where he was scrolling through the channels.

"Something G-rated, please," Maddy told him.

He glanced over and flashed her a grin. It was the first time Maddy had seen him smile.

"Don't worry," he said. "I won't broaden the little tyke's horizons while you're gone."

"I appreciate that," Maddy said.

"Tuck in my chin, Daddy," Riley said.

She crossed to the bed, leaning down to give Riley a kiss. "Tristan's going to stay with you while you sleep, honey."

"Okay, Mommy. Daddy says you're going to dance?"

"I'm going to dance." She glanced at Chase to find his gaze fixed on her chest. She realized her blouse had gaped open, and she was giving him a view of her white, lacy bra. She quickly straightened.

"How about *The Dog Who Saved Christmas*?" Tristan asked from where he sat at Riley's feet.

"It's summer," Riley said.

"It's a funny movie," Tristan said.

Riley looked to Maddy. "Can I *really* watch TV in bed?"

She ruffled his hair. "You can really watch TV in bed. But only because we're in a motel."

"Goody," Riley said, grinning as he wiggled up from under the covers.

He propped his head on a pillow. His cheeks were flushed, and his eyelids were droopy. She'd be surprised if he lasted through the opening credits.

"Thanks," she said to Tristan.

Tristan jabbed a thumb in Chase's direction. "Thank him. I'm getting triple meat, double cheese, and a contribution to my new cell phone."

"I'll make sure I do."

Then Maddy caught Chase's hungry gaze.

She hadn't meant the words to sound sexy. But they had. A shot of pure arousal raised tingling goose bumps on her skin. A pulse pinged low in her abdomen.

Dancing. It was nothing but dancing tonight.

Chase opened the door and she walked past him onto the breezeway. The air was sultry warm, the wind still, traffic below whizzing past under the streetlights. The big motel sign was yellow, bathing everything in a soft glow.

Then the door shut behind them and they were alone.

He looked to the left, and then to the right, then he pressed her against the painted concrete wall and kissed her thoroughly. She was instantly awash in passion. She'd missed him so much.

She wrapped her arms around his neck and absorbed the feel of his hard body against hers. The kiss was long and intimate and amazing.

"I want you so bad," he whispered against her mouth.

"I know," she said.

"I've missed you so much."

"I've missed you too."

A voice sounded below them. A car door slammed, and he backed slightly away.

"It can't be tonight, can it?" he said.

"It can't be tonight." She wished it could.

But there were too many people around them. Piper and Tristan were right next door. And she and Riley were sharing a bed. It couldn't possibly be tonight.

The door to Piper's room opened and Chase took a big step back.

"You look terrific," he told Piper as she emerged.

She did a pirouette. Her jeans were black. She wore rhinestone high heels. Her hair was in a messy updo. And her sheer, blue blouse was unbuttoned halfway to reveal a lacy pink camisole.

Maddy suddenly felt dowdy.

"My truck's in the parking lot," Chase said, gesturing for Piper to go first.

As Maddy started to walk behind Piper, Chase clasped her upper arm, slowing her down.

"You look fantastic," he whispered in her ear. "Nobody there is going to hold a candle to you."

A little glow grew in her heart. She felt like she was on a date again. She liked the feeling.

Chapter Eight

CHASE TOLD HIMSELF to enjoy what he had and quit wishing for more. Maddy was in his arms. She was smiling and she was perfectly in sync with his steps.

The local band was pretty good, and it was Chase and Maddy's second dance together. He was going to have to let her go soon if he didn't want to make his interest too obvious. Zane was in the room. He'd sent them a wave while he danced with a cute, curvy blonde in a white, rhinestone decorated cowboy hat.

"What's Eli doing here?" There was surprise in Maddy's voice.

The appearance of her second brother meant it was definitely time to back off. Chase stopped dancing and guided her to the edge of the floor.

"My brother Eli is here," she elaborated. "That's him over by the bar."

Chase considered his response. He wasn't going to lie to her, but he didn't want to step on any family toes either. They obviously hadn't yet told her about the plan to buy the Douglas Ranch.

"I met him earlier," Chase said.

She whirled her head to look at Chase. "You *did?*"

"Zane introduced us."

"I guess they didn't know I was coming."

Eli spotted them and started to approach. His gaze on Chase was anything but friendly. It said back off. No, it said back *the hell* off.

"They didn't know you'd be here," Chase said.

"I suppose," she said. "Is there something special about Zane's ride this weekend?"

Chase let that one pass, assuming she didn't expect an answer from him.

"Hey, Button." Eli's smile for Maddy was warm. He lifted her off the floor in a hug.

"What are you doing here?" she asked him.

"Watching my little brother ride bulls. What are you doing here? What are you doing with *him?*" As he set her down, Eli canted his head toward Chase.

"Dancing. Tell me what's going on with you. How's the job? I haven't heard from you in ages."

"The job's good," Eli said, all but shouldering Chase out of the way.

"Think I'll get a drink," Chase said. He had no desire to get into a contest with Eli over the rights to Maddy.

"A beer for me," Maddy said, clearly making the assumption he'd be coming back. "Whatever they have on tap."

"You got it," said Chase, catching Eli's frown.

Chase's plan was give them some space to keep Eli from getting suspicious. But that sure hadn't worked out.

Piper fell into step beside him. "Is that Eli Merrick?"

The question surprised Chase. "I thought you knew the family."

"I do. I did. But it's been years since I saw anyone but Maddy and Zane. He's bigger than he used to be."

"He's a big guy, alright."

"Does he know about you and Maddy?"

Chase wasn't sure what she was getting at. "You mean about Riley thinking I'm the other Chase?"

"No." Piper shook her head. "That's not what I mean."

Chase wasn't about to give anything away. He couldn't tell if Piper actually knew something or if she was just fishing for information.

"Maddy told me," Piper said.

Chase wasn't falling for that either. "Told you what?"

Piper stopped dead still.

He turned to see the blood drain from her face.

"What's wrong?"

"Is that Lucas?"

Chase looked. "Yes."

Piper grabbed his arm. "Get me out of here."

"What? Why?"

"Just do it. Walk me to the door." She started to move, all but dragging him along.

Chase saw no other choice. "You don't want to see Lucas."

"Yes. No. I don't." She seemed genuinely rattled.

"What's the problem?"

"Nothing. It's no big deal."

It was pretty obvious to Chase that it was a big deal. He waited for her to elaborate.

"It's just that we had an ugly fight years ago, and I don't want to re-hash it here tonight."

"You think he'd do that?" Chase couldn't see it. From what he knew of Lucas, Lucas was refined and circumspect.

"Yes, I think he'd do exactly that." She glanced surreptitiously behind them as they walked.

Now she had Chase curious. "How long has it been since you saw him?"

"For a minute at Maddy's. Before that it was high school."

"I think you're overreacting." Chase didn't want to leave the party. He wouldn't leave Piper or any woman to her own devices, but he had no intention of leaving Maddy behind either.

"He's coming." Piper's voice was almost a squeak.

"Did he see you?" It was Chase's turn to glance back.

Lucas had seen her alright. He was barreling down on them with laser focus, anger tightening his expression.

"Are you *sure* it's been more than a decade?" Chase asked.

"I'm sure."

"What are *you* doing here?" Lucas demanded of Piper.

"Hello, Lucas," Chase said, hoping the man wasn't going to cause a scene.

"We need to talk," Lucas said to Piper, his eyes hard as blue steel.

"No, we don't," Piper said.

"Outside, now."

Chase couldn't stand by. "She said no, Lucas. Come on, man."

"This is none of your concern." Lucas didn't even look his way.

"She came with me," Chase said.

Lucas rounded on him. "She *what*?"

"Both her and Maddy came with me."

"Then she's not your date," Lucas stated.

"I'm not letting you drag her outside against her will."

"You're back in Deadwood," Lucas said in an accusatory tone.

Piper crossed her arms over her chest. "What if I am?"

Chase found his attention straying to Maddy. She was still with Eli. He found himself grateful for that. As long as she was with that bear of a brother, other guys weren't likely to hit on her.

"You picked Deadwood."

"Damn right I did."

"You know we have to talk," Lucas said.

"There's nothing left to say."

175

"Oh, yes, there is." Lucas was all but towering over her, shoulders forward, feet planted apart.

Chase took a half step in between them, facing Lucas. "You think you need to talk to her? Okay. It's fair to ask."

Lucas slid him an impatient glare.

Chase ignored it. "Here's a thought. Maybe you could try not intimidating her so bad?"

"I'm not—" Lucas closed his eyes and took a deep breath, moderating his tone. His stance relaxed, and he drew back. "Piper. It would be good if we talked."

"I'm not going outside with you." She sounded more annoyed than frightened now.

"I don't think you want to talk in here."

Piper hesitated.

"You have to know I won't give up."

Chase looked at her. If she still said no, he was walking her away. He'd take her back to the motel or wherever she wanted to go, no matter what it might do to his relationship with Lucas. He'd come back for Maddy.

"Fine," Piper said shortly.

"Are you sure?" Chase asked her, surprised.

"She agreed," Lucas said, his tone resolute. "Your duty is done."

Chase watched her expression a moment longer to be sure.

She put a hand on his arm. "It's fine. Thanks. But I'll be okay."

"Call me if you need me."

"She won't need you," Lucas said.

Chase took a step back, leaving them to it. Whatever it was they had to hash out, it was no longer any of his business.

He made his way back to the bar and ordered three beers. Eli was starting to look easy in comparison to his older brother.

"Hey, Chase." Zane leaned on the bar next to him. "How's it going?"

"Great," Chase said, relieved that at least one Merrick brother didn't seem to want a fist fight. "Looks like you're having a good time."

"I'm always having a good time."

"You're riding tomorrow?"

Zane wouldn't be the first cowboy to ride with a hangover, but Chase sure didn't recommend it.

"I'll be fine by noon." Zane clapped him on the shoulder. "Until then, Miss Harvest Homecoming seems to want to keep me company."

"The blonde in the white hat?"

"That's the one."

"Are you sure she's over eighteen?"

"She's twenty."

"You might want to check her ID."

Zane laughed. "Way ahead of you, buddy."

Chase shook his head. He couldn't remember ever being

BARBARA DUNLOP

so carefree. He wasn't sure he'd have wanted it that way. Though, looking back, maybe he should have played the field a while before settling on Laura-Leigh. For sure, Laura-Leigh should have looked around before she said yes to Chase.

Come to think of it, she had looked around. She just hadn't bothered telling Chase she was doing it.

"When are you going to tell Maddy?" Chase asked Zane.

"Tell her what?"

"About the Douglas Ranch. What else? Are you keeping other things from her?"

"Hundreds," Zane said. "For instance, Miss Harvest Homecoming."

"I doubt your sister cares about Miss Harvest Homecoming."

"I agree," Zane said with authority.

The bartender set three mugs of beer in front of Chase, and he handed the man a twenty.

"She'll care about the Douglas Ranch. I assume you're planning to sell the house for the down payment."

"We'll have to."

"Then you better tell her she's moving."

"I'm leaving that to Lucas," Zane said.

Chase thought that was probably a smart approach, although Lucas seemed pretty distracted at the moment.

"Don't let him wait too long," Chase said.

"On it," Zane said, but his attention had already wandered to Miss Harvest Homecoming. He took his beer and left.

Chase left a tip for the bartender and gathered up the mugs, making his way back across the crowded floor to Maddy and Eli. By the time he got there, Wyatt had joined the conversation.

"…a family reunion without me?" Maddy was saying.

"You're here," Wyatt pointed out.

"You didn't know I was coming."

"Zane thought you were coming," Eli said.

Chase handed each of them a beer.

"Thanks," Maddy said.

Wyatt gave him a mock toast.

"It'll take more than a beer," Eli said to Chase.

"You're a tough sell, aren't you?" Chase returned.

"I'm not a pushover."

"Neither am I," Chase said. "But I am thirsty, so if you'll excuse me."

Before he could leave, Maddy linked her arm with his.

"I'm going with you. I'll leave the boys to their boys' club."

Chase didn't know whether to be pleased or worried. He decided to go with pleased. Eli could stew in his own annoyance. Chase had Maddy to himself again.

"They're always like that," she complained as they walked.

"Like what?"

"No girls allowed. They used to exclude me from everything."

"They all seem to love you very much."

"Like I'm a china doll." She frowned over the words.

"You're pretty as a china doll," he offered.

"I'm not delicate." She stumbled, and he quickly grabbed her and steadied her. "And I don't need help."

He raised a mocking brow. "*Really?*"

"*That* was a loose floorboard. Not my fault."

"I think you're the perfect combination of delicate and tough."

She gave a bright, slightly glassy smile and leaned against him as they walked. "What a nice thing to say."

"You've had more than just beer, haven't you?"

"Piper and I had a few shots when we first got here."

"It's not smart to get drunk at a party full of rowdy cowboys."

"Since three of those cowboys are my brothers, and one is…" She paused. "You. I think I'm safe."

"Just don't make a habit of it." He hated the thought of her drinking while he wasn't around.

"I don't. And I'm not drunk. It was a loose floorboard, and you should stop being a killjoy."

"Is that what I'm being?"

"I'm a single mom. I don't get out very often. I just want to kick back."

He couldn't say he blamed her for that. It was easy to see

that taking care of a three-year-old was a full time job. And she was doing it brilliantly.

"Kick back away," he said. "You want another shot?"

"Okay, now you're trying to get me drunk."

"I can see I'm not going to win in this conversation."

"You've already won."

"I have?" He was dying to know what she meant by that.

"Did you miss the part last week where we had great sex?"

He had absolutely not missed that part. He'd been thinking about it ever since. "You might want to keep your voice down."

She dropped her voice to a stage whisper. "That was a win."

"I didn't know it was a contest."

"It was a win-win." She chuckled, seeming to like her joke.

They were weaving their way between clusters of people, heading in the general direction of the bar. But he was in no hurry to get there.

"You really think anyone's going to overhear me with that band playing?"

He supposed he didn't. "Did you tell Piper we slept together?"

"I may have mentioned it on the drive over. Piper's cool. She won't tell anyone."

"What about your brothers?"

Maddy shook her head. "They're a bit... well... funny about me."

"No kidding." Chase couldn't help but picture Eli.

"They're protective."

"That first day we met, the second Lucas got me alone, he flat out ordered me not to sleep with you."

"Seriously?"

"Yes."

"Do guys do that? I mean, when they don't even know each other?"

"They do when it's their sister."

She went quiet.

They came to the bar and he ordered a beer. When it came, he switched, giving her the cold one.

"I'm sorry about Lucas," she said.

Chase couldn't help but smile. "It's not your fault. You slept with me anyway."

"No. *You* slept with *me* anyway."

"I suppose I did."

She gave him a suggestive grin, and he wanted to drag her into his arms right then and there. He took a swig of the beer instead.

She scanned the crowded room. "Do you know what happened to Piper?"

"She went outside with Lucas."

"She *did?*" Maddy seemed surprised. "Wait a minute, Lucas is here too?"

"He is." Chase moved the conversation on. "Do you happen to know what's going on between those two?"

Maddy shook her head. "Piper said they had a fight. But that was years and years ago."

"She told me the same thing."

"Do you think we should rescue her?" Maddy asked.

"That's not my area of expertise."

"I think we should rescue her."

Chase supposed Lucas had had ample time to say whatever he wanted.

"Are you ready to leave then?" Truth was, he would happily get out of here, away from the noise, away from the crowds, and away from Maddy's brothers.

"I'm ready," she said.

He took a final drink of the beer then put his hand on the small of her back to guide her to the door.

They found Piper outside, perched on a concrete retaining wall, gazing across the crowded parking lot. Lucas wasn't around.

"Is everything okay?" Maddy asked as they approached. Her cheeks were flushed and her eyes were bright under the porch lights.

It was probably the shots, but Chase couldn't help appreciating her beauty all over again.

"It's fine," Piper said, putting on what looked like a stoic expression and coming to her feet.

"Where's Lucas?" Maddy glanced at the few clusters of

conversation groups.

Piper shrugged. "Are we going back to the motel now?"

"Is that what you want?" Chase asked her.

"I've had enough party for tonight," she said, turning toward the spot where Chase had parked the truck.

He took a last look behind them to see if any Merrick brothers were following. They weren't.

BACK AT THE motel, they relieved Tristan. Riley was asleep in the middle of the bed, and Chase knew he should head for his own room. But he wasn't ready to leave Maddy just yet.

"Daddy?" Riley asked in a sleepy voice, shifting under the covers.

Chase smiled resignedly, banishing hopes of a passionate good night kiss. He sat down on the edge of the bed. "I'm here, buckaroo."

"Will you read me a story, Daddy?"

Chase gave Maddy a questioning gaze, wondering if she had brought along any books. She gave a little shake of her head.

"We don't have your books here," he told Riley, tucking the covers up around his chin.

"Can you make up a story? Sometimes Mommy makes up my stories."

"Mommy's here too," Chase said.

"I want a Daddy story. A horse story."

Chase realized Riley was coming more and more awake. He wanted to keep him sleepy. A story seemed like the best way to do that.

"Okay," Chase told him soothingly, stretching his legs out on the bed to get comfortable. "Once upon a time…"

Maddy gave an amused smile at the opening words, and Chase responded with a shrug. He was operating on the fly here.

"There was a little boy who had a painted pony named Trigger."

"What color was the pony?"

"It was black and white. And it's time for you to be quiet and listen."

"Okay, Daddy."

"Close your eyes."

Riley closed his eyes.

"The boy's name was Henry. Henry and Trigger lived on a ranch in Montana in a little house among the rolling hills, green grass, and aspen trees. Trigger was a naughty pony."

Riley smiled.

"Trigger loved oats. Henry's daddy kept the oats locked up in the back of the barn. But one day, Henry forgot to shut Trigger's stall door."

While Chase talked, saying whatever came into his mind about the barn and the pony and boy, Maddy left for the small bathroom.

She emerged a few minutes later in her T-shirt and pajama bottoms, climbing into the bed on the opposite side of Riley.

"The door was latched," Chase said, watching Maddy as he spoke, "but Trigger could smell the oats through the little crack between the door and the barn wall."

She smiled and lay her head down on the pillow, closing her eyes.

It was distracting to have her so close. But now wasn't the time for anything beyond appreciating her company. So he kept talking, introducing a kitten into the plot and describing its antics at length.

As his voice droned on, both Riley and Maddy drifted off.

When he was sure Riley was deep asleep, Chase stopped talking and turned off the bedside lamp. Pale light filtered in through the sheers on the window. He rose, rounding the end of the bed, coming down on one knee at Maddy's side. There he smiled at her flushed cheeks and brushed a lock of her hair back from her temple.

She opened her eyes. She smiled back at him.

"Hi, there," he said.

"I fell asleep."

"I didn't mean to wake you."

"You didn't."

He grinned at that. "You're awake, aren't you?"

"Unless I'm dreaming."

He couldn't stop himself from asking, "Is it a good dream?"

She put her hand over his. "It's a great dream."

He leaned in and kissed her lips. "I'd give anything to stay."

"Don't go yet."

"Okay." He eased himself to a sitting position on the floor beside her, still holding her hand.

"I didn't expect to see you here," she said.

"Did Riley talk you into coming?"

"He did. And Piper. Tristan was angling to go to a party, and she thought it would be better to get him out of town."

Chase twined his fingers with hers. "I thought it was going to be better if I stayed away."

"And was it?"

"Not for me. Was it for you? For Riley?"

"I missed you," she said. "Nothing's changed with Riley."

Chase brought her knuckles to his lips and gave them a kiss. "What are we going to do?"

"I don't know. Never tell him? Get married and pretend everything is normal?"

Her tone was light, words joking, but something hardened in Chase's chest. His reaction was visceral. No way, no how would he be the stand-in for another man. For a moment, he couldn't breathe.

"I'm joking, Chase."

"I know you're joking." He rolled to his feet. "But I should go."

"Chase?" She sat up.

"Go back to sleep."

"Don't leave like this."

"It's late." He had to get out of here. He had to think.

She climbed out of bed.

"Maddy, don't."

She put her arms around him, and he couldn't stop himself from hugging her back.

"I'm so sorry," she said, her voice filled with regret.

He fought against the arousal that was battling with his better sense. "You don't have to be sorry about anything. You said it yourself. It's nobody's fault. It just is."

"It was stupid to make a joke. I shouldn't have said it."

"Quit worrying. Go to sleep. Riley will wake up early."

Chase stepped back from her. His body felt like lead as he walked to the door. He should have known better than to play at this game.

She might think she wanted him. But it wasn't him. It had never been him. What she wanted, what she deserved, was to put her life back together. She wanted what she'd lost, her husband, Riley's real father. And who could blame her? Of course that was what she wanted.

Closing the door silently behind him, he turned on the breezeway to find Eli striding straight towards him.

The two men stopped.

Eli gave a cold exclamation of disgust. "Tell me again how you're not sleeping with my sister."

Chase moved from the door to keep Maddy from overhearing.

"I was telling Riley a story," he said, wondering why he was bothering with an explanation.

"Sure, you were," Eli's skepticism rang through his low tone as he pointedly glanced at his watch.

"Believe whatever you want." Chase was in no mood to defend his behavior to Eli or anyone else.

"I will." Eli firmed his stance, his glare a challenge.

"You don't want to fight me," Chase said.

"No, *you* don't want to fight *me*."

"Don't do this, man."

"I once stood blindly by while a man took advantage of her," Eli said. "I'm not going to stand by again."

"She's not eighteen anymore."

Eli moved closer. "*That's* your excuse."

Chase could see what was happening here. "You do know you're pissed at him and not at me."

"I'm pissed at *you*."

It occurred to Chase then that Eli had a right to be pissed at him. He hadn't made love to Maddy tonight, but he had made love to her. And though he hadn't done it on purpose, he had taken advantage of her vulnerability. She'd been tired, afraid and lonely, and Chase had swooped right in.

They said confession was good for the soul. And Chase's

soul needed something.

He opened his mouth, knowing full well how Eli was likely to react. "It didn't happen tonight. But I have slept with her."

"You son-of-a-bitch." As expected, Eli's meaty fist instantly connected with Chase's chin.

Chase staggered from the powerful blow. He clamped down on the reflex to defend himself. The punch felt right. Chase knew he'd deserved it.

"Probably good that you got that over with," he said. "I think we both feel better."

Before Eli could erase the look of confusion on his face, Chase brushed past him to his own room.

As Maddy and Piper walked through the concession area at the fairgrounds, Riley skipping between them, Maddy couldn't help keeping an eye out for Chase. She wanted to assure herself that everything was okay, but she was very much afraid that it wasn't. In fact, she was positive that it wasn't.

"You're quiet," Piper said.

Maddy tried to shake off the feeling of dread. "I'm tired."

"We didn't stay out that late."

"Riley woke up when I got home." Maddy didn't add

that she'd lain awake for hours after Riley had gone back to sleep and Chase had left, reliving the moment over and over again.

She was terrified she'd scared him off, that she'd come across as pathetic, desperate, and obsessive. She'd give anything to take back her words, those ten seconds when she'd made such a colossal mistake.

"Daddy!" Riley cried, interrupting her thoughts.

He immediately set off in a trot.

Chase looked surprised. He hesitated for a moment, but then he smiled back at Riley.

Cold rushed through Maddy and her feet stopped moving.

Piper turned back. "What is wrong?"

Chase swung Riley up into his arms.

"I made a joke," Maddy said.

"So?"

"About getting married. He didn't take it well."

"To Chase?"

"Who else?"

"Last night?"

He was coming closer and Maddy had to stop talking. Chase smiled at them, but his expression was guarded, and he didn't meet her eyes. The intimacy from last night completely was gone. He looked remote.

There was a shadow of a bruise on his chin, and she didn't want to think about where he might have gone after he left her.

"Hi, Maddy," he said. "Hello, Piper."

"Daddy, we're goin' to the bull pens." Riley wiggled in Chase's arms. "Wanna come?"

"Sure, buckaroo. I'll come along."

Chase's tone was even. She couldn't say he was angry or upset, but something was definitely off.

"You two go ahead," Piper said to Chase. "Maddy and I are grabbing a coffee."

"You bet," Chase said, hoisting Riley up onto his shoulders as he turned away.

Riley squealed in delight. "I'm *big*."

"Point me to the bulls," Chase said as he started to walk.

Riley pointed. "That way, Daddy. The clown has balloons." He rocked on Chase's shoulders like he was riding a horse. Maddy thought her heart would break in two.

"You look totally freaked out," Piper said. "What happened? What was the joke?"

Maddy didn't want to share the embarrassing incident, but she had to talk to someone. "We were talking about Riley, what to do about telling him the truth. And I blurted out—I was tired, I'd been drinking. I don't know what I was thinking."

"What did you say?"

"I said maybe we shouldn't tell him. Maybe we should just get married instead."

Piper didn't respond.

"I *know*," Maddy all but wailed. "I'm an idiot. I scared him half to death. He bolted from the room, and now he won't even look at me."

"Were you serious?" Piper asked. "Do you really think not telling Riley is a viable option?"

"Of course I don't think that. It's absurd."

"But Chase thought you were testing the waters."

Maddy closed her eyes for a moment. "I want to die. I honestly want the ground to swallow me up and be done with it."

"Exactly how into this guy are you?" Piper pointed to a concession stand serving coffee and cinnamon doughnuts.

"This isn't about me," Maddy said, allowing herself to be directed. "It's about Riley."

"You can't still believe that."

"It's mostly about Riley."

Piper glanced behind them in the direction Chase had walked. "I don't think you have to worry about Riley. Chase is being an exceptionally good—"

"There it is," Maddy said. "It's like he's his real father. In fact, he's better than his real father."

"That's a dangerous path," Piper said as they joined the short lineup.

"I know. And I'm going to stop. Right now."

There was no way she could bring herself to admit it out loud, but last night Maddy had only been half joking. She was falling for Chase, and she was falling very hard.

Chapter Nine

ESIDE THE FENCED bull enclosure, Chase held fast to Riley's hand.

"My sister do that?" Zane asked, checking out Chase's jaw.

"Yeah, right."

"Is he gnarly, Uncle Zane?" Riley asked, peering through the fence at a white brahma bull named High Hume.

"He's gnarly," Zane confirmed with a smile.

"You gonna ride him?" Riley asked.

"Maybe tomorrow," Zane said. "What happened?" he asked Chase.

"They sawed off his horns," Riley said. "Does it hurt when they do that?"

"No," Chase said, preferring Riley's question to Zane's. "It's like cutting your hair."

"Pretty fat hair," Riley said, chuckling at his own joke.

Zane smiled too. "Bar fight?" he tossed another guess out to Chase.

"No big deal," Chase said.

If Eli hadn't told Zane about the incident, Chase had no

intention of being the one to bring him up to speed. As far as Chase was concerned, the rest of the family could remain in the dark.

He caught a glimpse of Piper coming through the crowd, and immediately glanced around for Maddy.

"One, two, three," Riley said.

"Who hit you?" Zane asked, obviously getting impatient.

Chase gave up. "Eli."

Zane drew back in obvious shock. "Eli *hit* you?"

"It was no big deal. We worked it out."

"You hit him back?"

"Five spots," Riley said. "The white bull has five spots."

Piper was coming closer, but Chase couldn't see Maddy.

He wanted to see her again. He wanted to hold her again. And he desperately wanted to be wrong.

But he wasn't wrong. She was transferring her affection in a perfectly reasonable way. She didn't even know she was doing it. If he'd learned anything from Laura-Leigh, it was that a person couldn't force love.

They could pretend for a while, but eventually the truth came out. And this time, it was more than just Chase who would get hurt. It would be Riley as well.

Chase couldn't help but glance down at him. He was coming to love the kid.

Riley held up a spread fingered hand. "Five spots, Daddy."

Chase ruffled his hair, his heart swelling his chest. "You

got that right."

"Chase?" Zane prompted.

"Let it go," Chase said. "Hi, Piper."

"Hi, Chase," Piper returned. "Hi, Zane. Maddy asked me to take Riley for a while. She's going to meet us back at the motel."

"Something wrong?" Chase asked, because he couldn't help himself.

"She's tired is all," Piper said. "Riley had her up early."

"He does that," Chase said, his gaze dropping down again. "Why don't you leave him with me for a while?"

Piper looked uncertain.

"I promised him we'd get a balloon." Chase knew his time with Riley was limited, and he didn't want to give up the whole rest of the afternoon. "We can kick around the kid zone and grab a hotdog."

"I supposed that would work," Piper said. "I should probably track Tristan down anyway."

"Zane can help," Chase said.

"Say what?" Zane's attention seemed to perk up.

"Help the lady out," Chase said. "She needs to make sure her teenage son isn't getting into any trouble. Maybe he'd like to try steer riding."

Zane grinned at the suggestion.

Piper frowned. "He grew up in Chicago."

"I'll make a man out of him," Zane said.

"I'm not going to let you hurt my son."

Zane waved a dismissive hand. "It's harmless. There's a first-timer's category. Docile steers. It'll give him bragging rights when he gets back home."

Piper hesitated.

Zane took her arm. "Let's go find him. At least give him a chance to decide for himself."

"Fine." Piper gave in. "This should be interesting."

Zane shot Chase a conspiratorial grin as they walked away.

Chase knew Zane wouldn't let Tristan get seriously hurt. But if the kid agreed to ride a steer, he was going to get bumped and bruised. From what Chase had seen so far, it wouldn't do Tristan any harm to get out there and challenge himself.

Chase crouched down so he was eye-level with Riley. "Which one's your favorite?" he asked, canting his head to the pens of bulls.

"The black one," said Riley. "He looks mean, but he looks smart."

"He looks smart?"

"When I stare into his eyes, he twitches his tail."

"You know it's very dangerous to approach a bull, right?"

Riley gave a solemn nod. "They're sneaky bastards."

"Did Uncle Zane tell you that?"

"I don't know."

"You can't say bastards around your mom."

"Okay."

"Or around any ladies."

"Okay, Daddy."

Chase was new to this parenting thing, so he was making it up as he went along. "Really, it's probably not a word you should use. Bull riders sometimes use inappropriate language."

Riley seemed to be considering Chase's words carefully.

Chase was proud of the way he was handling the small infraction. He waited a moment, letting his advice sink in.

"Can we get ice cream?" Riley asked. "I like the swirly white and chocolate kind with sprinkles."

Chase was forced to rethink his self-satisfaction, so much for his advice sinking in. Maybe this parenting thing was trickier than he thought. However, he did know ice cream on an empty stomach would be bad news.

"How about a hotdog first?" he asked.

"A chili cheese dog!" Riley took his hand.

"Easy there, buckaroo." Chase wasn't sure a chili cheese dog was any better on a three-year-old's stomach than ice cream. "Have you ever had a chili cheese dog?"

"Uncle Zane says they're the bomb."

"How about a little ketchup instead?"

"I like ketchup."

Chase rose. "One hotdog with ketchup it is."

The two started for the concession area and a cluster of small tables with plaid plastic table cloths and folding chairs. The crowds were thick midafternoon. They'd grown as people showed up to claim their seats and pick up concession food for dinner. The music would grow louder. The lights would come on. And the beer garden and VIP sponsor areas would fill up with those who liked to socialize.

Chase couldn't help but wish he was riding.

He'd like to make a good ride with Maddy and Riley in the audience. He'd like to impress them.

His steps slowed as he realized that for the first time since leaving the Twin River Valley, he wasn't seeing riding as a balm to his anger. He'd barely thought about Laura-Leigh since arriving in Deadwood.

Now he thought about Maddy instead. And there was definitely no anger there.

"Look, Daddy." Riley's voice was excited. "It's you in the picture."

Chase glanced to a row of posters along a board fence. They depicted previous AEBR champions, year by year.

Riley surged closer. But the poster he pointed to wasn't of Chase. It was his father riding Road to Ruin. The bull was three feet off the round, Chase Barrett's hat was low, his arm extended, his knees bent in a perfect pose. He'd been one hell of a rider.

It took Chase a moment to realize that Riley had gone quiet.

Riley leaned into Chase's leg, wrapping his arms around it.

Chase's stomach contracted. He crouched down on one

knee.

"Hey," he said gently to Riley.

"Is that my other daddy?" Riley asked in a small voice, pointing to the poster.

Anxiety coursed through Chase. He knew he had mere seconds to get this right.

"That's your first daddy," he said.

"He's dead?" Riley asked.

"I'm afraid so." Chase put an arm around Riley's small shoulders. "He's in heaven now. He can't ever come back."

A beat went by in silence while Riley seemed to digest the information.

"Uncle Zane says there are bulls to ride in heaven."

"I'm sure there are," Chase said, struggling to find the right direction to take the conversation. "I bet your daddy is riding one right now."

Riley slipped up onto Chase's bent knee. "Are you my new daddy?"

Chase had been thrown, twisted, butted and stomped more times than he could count, but he'd never felt pain like this.

"We haven't worked everything out yet," he said, his throat thickening over the words. "But I'll always be your friend. You can count on me whenever you need me, Riley. I promise you that."

"'Kay," Riley said softly. He twisted the fabric of Chase's shirt cuff between his little fingers.

"You know your mommy loves you, right?" Chase asked.

"I know."

"And Uncle Zane and Lucas and Eli and Wyatt. There are loads of people who love you and are going to take good care of you."

"Do you love me, Daddy?"

"Yes, I do," Chase answered honestly. He gave Riley a squeeze. "I love you a whole lot, buckaroo."

Riley fell silent, and Chase waited.

"My other daddy."

Chase held his breath, afraid of what Riley was going to ask.

"He didn't know how to paint a bike," Riley said.

Chase strongly doubted that, but he couldn't help a small smile of relief. Bike painting seemed like a harmless topic.

"Can we paint it orange next time?" Riley asked.

"Sure," Chase said. He had no idea how they'd work out the details. But he promised himself when the time came he'd move heaven and earth to paint Riley's bike orange.

"Do you think they'll have orange soda?" Riley asked, his voice sounding more normal.

"Who?"

"At the hotdog place. Do you think they'll have orange soda?"

"I'm sure they will."

"Can I have orange soda?"

"Absolutely."

"It turns my tongue orange." Riley sounded quite proud of the pronouncement and stuck out his tongue as a further demonstration as he slipped off Chase's knee.

"Orange tongue it is," Chase said, relieved and impressed by how well Riley had handled the revelation that Chase wasn't his real father.

He wanted to rush off and tell Maddy the news. But he didn't want Riley to see him making a big deal about it. Going with the flow, keeping things low key and ordinary for the next couple of hours seemed like it would be the best thing for the little boy.

MADDY AWOKE WITH a vague feeling of disquiet. It took her a moment, but then she remembered the remote expression on Chase's face at the fairgrounds, the distance he was keeping between them. She'd made such a foolish mistake.

Her headache was gone, but her heartache was still in full force. She glanced at the clock to see it was nearly five. She was grateful to Piper for babysitting for so long.

Maddy sat up and swung her legs from beneath the covers. She was wearing the shorts and T-shirt she'd dressed in this morning. They were rumpled, but good enough to pick up Riley next door. She took a drink of water, ran her fingers through her hair, then headed onto the breezeway to Piper's room.

She knocked, and Piper was quick to open up.

"Feel better?" Piper asked her, drawing the door wide.

Riley was on the floor of the motel room engrossed in a game involving his mini racers and a deck of cards from the casino.

"The headache's gone."

"That's good." Piper closed the door behind her, drawing Maddy to one side, her expression earnest.

"What's going on?" Maddy asked, taking another look at Riley to make sure he seemed okay.

"Chase says Riley knows," Piper whispered.

"Knows what?"

"The big what," said Piper. "He saw some kind of poster with Chase Barrett on it, and he realized Chase wasn't Chase."

Maddy looked immediately to Riley. "How did he take it? Was he upset?"

"Chase said he took it like a trooper."

Maddy moved to Riley, sitting down on the floor next to his game. "Hi, honey."

"Hi, Mommy. The red car came in first. The blue one had a breakdown."

"They're racing?" Maddy asked, unsure of exactly what she should do. Should she bring it up? Wait for Riley to bring it up?

He made motor noises with his mouth.

"Did you have some lunch?" she asked.

"Daddy bought me a hotdog. It had ketchup, but no chili cheese. I had orange soda." He stuck out his tongue to prove it.

"Your tongue's orange," she observed, guessing that was what he expected her to say.

He grinned and went back to his racers.

She looked back to Piper. "I need to talk to Chase." She needed to know exactly what had happened.

"I think he's in his room. He just brought Riley back."

"Just now?" Maddy rechecked her watch. It had been nearly four hours.

"It sounds like they had fun together."

Maddy frowned. "And shared secrets."

"Maddy. I'm sure Chase didn't do it on purpose."

Maddy came to her feet. "I need to know."

"Of course you do. Go. Go, he's fine here for as long as you need."

Maddy turned her attention back to her son. "I need to go out for a few more minutes, honey," she told him.

"Bye-bye, Mommy."

"You can stay here with Piper."

"Tristan is addicted to his phone," Riley said.

"He told you that?" Maddy asked, continuing to be astonished at Riley's carefree mood. She had about a thousand questions rolling around in her head.

"Piper said so."

"Zane tried to get him to go steer riding."

Maddy blinked at Piper. "Seriously?"

"He refused."

"I don't blame him. Tristan had probably never even touched a steer, never mind ridden one."

"Zane says he's going to try again tomorrow."

"Zane needs to mind his own business." In Maddy's mind, it was downright mean to try to force Tristan into something he'd certainly fail at, and probably get hurt in the process.

"I'm not so sure," Piper said.

"You *want* Tristan to ride a steer?"

"He needs to grow up sometime."

"He'll get hurt."

"They have a first-timer's category."

"You're the worst mom ever," Maddy said. She couldn't imagine letting Riley do something so risky.

"Tristan is fifteen, not four. He needs a few knocks and bruises."

"Did you read that in a book somewhere?"

"You'll get there," Piper said. "Now go. Find out what happened with Chase."

"Yes," Maddy agreed.

She was annoyed with Chase when she left Piper's room, for undertaking such a momentous discussion without her. But halfway down the breezeway, the annoyance turned to acceptance. Whatever had happened, Riley didn't seem to have suffered any emotional trauma. And she couldn't imagine Chase had broached the subject on purpose.

By the time she got to Chase's room, her acceptance had turned to gratitude. Thanks to Chase, one of her biggest worries was resolved. And Riley seemed completely fine.

She knocked.

When he opened the door, she drank in the sight of him. His shirt was unbuttoned, his jeans riding low, his feet bare. His expression was still guarded, and the distance made her want to cry.

"I'm sorry," he said. "I didn't see it coming."

"No." She gave her head a definitive shake. "I'm here to thank you. Thank you, Chase."

She couldn't stop herself. She stepped in and wrapped her arms around him, laying her cheek against his chest. "Thank you so much."

The door swung shut behind her.

"Maddy." His voice was strained.

"I don't know what you did, but it was right, and I'm so incredibly grateful."

"You don't…" He rasped in a deep breath. "I can't…"

She looked up.

"Oh, hell." His arms went around her and his lips swooped down to hers.

She all but melted under his kiss. Memories of their lovemaking kicked in, desire and passion cascading through her. She opened to him, parting her lips, her tongue tangling with his.

His hands, warm and strong, callused and steady, slipped under her thin T-shirt, stroking her lower back. She stepped closer, her hips pressing against his thighs.

He groaned and his hands dropped to her rear, pulling her intimately into the vee of his thighs. Desperate to get closer still, she stripped off her shirt. They met skin to skin. He flicked open her bra and it fell away. Her nipples tingled against his chest.

"I've missed you so much," she whispered against his mouth.

"You're all I can think about." He scooped her into his arms, crossing the few steps to the bed.

There he sat down, her in his lap, and his hands closed over her breasts.

"Chase," she gasped.

His kisses deepened.

It was hot, and she was dying for him. She scrambled out of her shorts and panties. Then she straddled his lap. The denim of his jeans grazed her tender skin. Her arousal ran deep and insistent.

He cradled her cheeks, kissing her swollen mouth, his lips hot and tender, his breath sweet as it fanned her face.

She'd never wanted like this. She'd never felt like this. She'd never known with such a deep, unwavering certainty that something was so absolutely right.

His gray eyes darkened and he turned her onto her back.

She pushed off his shirt, clinging to his strong shoulders. He kissed her neck, her shoulders, her breasts, making his way downward, tasting every tender spot on her body.

She squirmed. Then she gasped for air. She dug her fingers into his hair.

Then he was rising, stripping off his jeans, coming down on top of her, as she welcomed him with a moan of completion.

He stilled while pulses throbbed from her toes to her brain.

She tried to move, but he captured her hips, holding her still against the mattress.

"This," he said, looking straight into her eyes.

She could feel arousal pushing insistently through her.

"I'll remember this forever." And then he was moving and her world took flight.

Colors danced before her eyes, and sounds clanged in her ears. His hands were everywhere. His lips worshipped her. And his thrusts were strong and deep, perfectly timed, matching her wants, until her body exploded, shuddering, pulsing as pleasure overtook her.

She cried out his name, and he answered with hers, groaning his own completion as his weight settled on her, solid and reassuring.

After a few moments, he rolled so that she was on top. He held her close, and their breathing synchronized. Neither of them spoke as the bedside clock counted off the minutes towards the evening's rides.

Maddy had no desire to move. Her world was perfect, and she wanted to keep it that way as long as humanly possible.

"You awake?" Chase asked softly.

"Yes."

She would have liked to pretend she was asleep. Maybe they could have lain there for another hour or more. But she knew they couldn't. Real life was outside the motel room door waiting for them.

He shifted them again, lying her beside him. Then he came up on his side.

She focused on his handsome, sexy face. "What happened?"

"Riley saw a poster of his dad. At first he thought it was me. But I guess having us side by side showed him the truth."

"What did he do?" Maddy sat up, cross-legged, pulling the sheet across her lap.

"He asked if Chase was his first daddy. I told him yes."

Maddy's chest tightened to painful. "Was he upset?"

"He was thoughtful. He's one amazing kid, Maddy."

"I know he is." Whatever else Chase Barrett had done, together they had produced an extraordinary child.

"He asked me if I was his new daddy." There was something in Chase's expression. Something wasn't right.

A chill came over her, and she swallowed. "What did you

say?"

"I told him I would always be his friend." Chase sat up and stepped into his jeans. "We have to talk, Maddy."

She wanted to shout *no*. She wanted to shut him up. She wanted to throw herself into his arms and keep the magic between them alive for just a few more minutes.

Someone pounded forcefully on the door.

Maddy jumped.

"Chase!" came Eli's deep voice. "Open up."

Maddy felt the blood drain from her face. "Don't answer."

"I know you're in there," Eli called out.

"I have to answer," Chase said.

Maddy searched for an escape route. She spied the bathroom and darted for it.

"He already knows," Chase told her as she crossed the room.

Maddy didn't care what Eli did or did not know. Her brother was *not* catching her naked in Chase's hotel room.

BARE CHESTED, CHASE opened the door to Eli, prepared to take whatever angry words Eli felt he needed to throw, but not prepared to take another undefended punch. If Eli got physical again, Chase was fighting back.

Eli strode into the room. "What did you tell Zane?"

Chase was instantly off balance.

Eli didn't even seem to notice the messy bed and Chase's state of undress.

"Zane?" Chase asked.

"He thinks I've messed up the land deal. They all think I've messed up the land deal by taking a swing at you."

"You didn't." Chase would never hold that against Eli.

"You deserved it," Eli barked. "You know you deserved it."

"Eli, stop—"

"And you could have hit me back. You could have stood up like a man. You didn't need to go behind my back and destroy our chances with the Douglas Ranch—"

"Eli, *shut up*."

"I'm not going to—"

"*Maddy's here*." Chase canted his head to the closed bathroom door.

There was a whimper and a thud on the other side of the door.

Chase threw Eli an impatient look.

Eli might hate that Chase was sleeping with his sister. But a far worse thing would be Maddy overhearing her brothers had made a deal behind her back.

Eli stilled, his expression clouding. He was clearly stunned, and clearly debating exactly how angry he should be and for which reason.

"Maddy?" he called out to her, his calm voice at odds

with his angry expression. At the same time, he glared daggers at Chase, his expression saying their conversation was far from over.

"Come out here, Maddy," Eli said.

"Go away," she cried.

"I'm not mad."

"I don't care."

"I need to talk to her alone," Chase said to Eli.

He wasn't backing out of the Douglas Ranch deal because Eli had hit him. But he was backing out. The situation with Maddy was completely untenable.

He couldn't go into business with her brothers. It would be feeding into the impossible fantasy all three of them, Maddy, Riley, and even Chase had built up in their minds.

"We're all adults," Eli called to Maddy. To Chase he said, "She needs an explanation."

"Not from you."

Eli's tone turned authoritative. "Madeline, get out here."

The bathroom door cracked.

"Maddy, wait," Chase cautioned.

He needed for Eli to leave, not to elaborate. Events were running out of his control, and there was no way this conversation ended well for any of them.

But Eli was too quick. "Chase is buying a ranch with us."

The door yawned wider, and Maddy appeared wrapped in a white robe.

"That's why we're all here in Missoula," Eli said.

"I don't understand." Her gaze darted to Chase, her confusion clear.

Eli kept talking. "We're here to discuss the details of buying the Douglas Ranch in Marietta Montana."

"Eli," Chase interrupted. "I need to talk to Maddy alone."

"You're buying a ranch?" Maddy asked Chase.

"It's not that simple."

"We're not going to be able to buy our land back, Maddy," Eli said. "It's just a fact. I'm sorry, but it's not going to happen."

Maddy was still looking at Chase. He could see the hope in her eyes. He could even guess her thoughts. She was seeing herself and Chase and Riley living happily even after on a Montana ranch surrounded by her entire extended family. He understood why she'd want that. He also knew why it could never happen.

"The Douglas Ranch is a real opportunity," Eli said to her. "We can start over, together."

Chase stepped in front of Eli. He made his tone definitive, his gaze hard and unbending. "I need to talk to her *alone*."

Eli's eyes narrowed in response. "Why?"

"I'm asking you to back off."

"And I'm asking you what you want with my sister."

Chase didn't know how much more of this he could take. "To talk about our *relationship*."

Eli glanced at Maddy then his gaze pointedly took in the entire room. It stopped again on Chase. "That relationship had damn well better include a ring on her finger."

"*Eli!*" Maddy sounded appalled.

"We've already agreed she's an adult," Chase said to Eli.

"Eli, leave," Maddy said.

Eli was clearly unhappy, but he backed off. He left the motel room, slamming the door shut behind him.

Chase was out of time. He loved Maddy and the last thing he wanted to do was hurt her. But the truth was the truth, and he couldn't run away from it any longer.

"Chase?" Her question was hesitant.

He girded himself and turned.

"Please tell me what's going on." She tightened the lapels of the robe across her chest.

"We should sit down," he invited.

"I don't want to sit down."

"Okay." He had no choice but to plunge right in. "Maddy, I know you think you know how you feel."

Her tone was cautious. "How exactly do you think I feel?"

"You can picture it. And it's so close, you can almost taste it: the perfect life, the perfect happily ever after."

"I don't believe in perfect anything, Chase."

"You had a fantastic family. There's no denying, you had everything you wanted. And then you lost it. And it broke your heart. It would break anyone's heart."

Her gaze was growing more remote, her shields going up against him.

"You want it back," he said. "I get that. And along I came, looking just like him, and Riley fixated on me."

"I know you're not Chase, Chase."

"On one level, yes." He believed she did.

She took a step forward. "On every level. I know you're not my dead husband."

"Maddy—"

"Don't Maddy me. I'm not some delusional little ingénue desperate for any man to step into my life and make me whole."

"I never said—"

"You're telling me I don't know my own mind." She moved to the lone armchair and dropped down. "What you're saying is that I don't know how I feel."

Chase sat on the end of the bed facing her. "What I'm saying is that you've been through a lot. I can't even imagine how hard it's been for you. As desperate as Riley was for me to be—"

"I'm *not* a three-year-old child. I have *never* mixed the two of you up."

"I'm not saying that either. I'm saying that sometimes when you want something so badly to be true—"

"Save it, Chase. If you don't love me, or if you're not ready for a family, if being a father to Riley—"

"This is not about Riley. I love Riley. How could I not

215

love Riley?" Chase realized he'd give just about anything to take on the job of being Riley's father.

"This isn't about how I feel," Maddy said. "It's about how you feel or don't feel, isn't it?"

He didn't want to say it. It would hurt them both too much. But if that's what she needed... if that's what she needed to walk away, then he would.

"The way I feel..." he said, forcing out the words, "the way I truly feel is... I could never trust it. I could never know for sure it was real."

"I'm not her, Chase." Maddy's voice was stone cold.

She stood and crossed the small room to where she'd discarded her clothes, picking them up one by one. "I know she hurt you. I know she betrayed you. But I'm *not* her. And I'm *never* going to do that." She stepped into her panties then into her shorts. "But if that's not enough for you, then I think I can guess where you stand."

Chase wanted to shout that she didn't know where he stood. He was madly in love with her. It was going to kill him to walk away. But it was better that it happened now, because it was going to be worse later.

It would be worse for Riley and worse for Maddy, because she was going to cling to her fantasy to the bitter end. She was kind, and she was caring, and she wasn't going to want to let it fall apart. He had to be strong and walk away now.

She shrugged into her T-shirt. "Will you at least say

goodbye to my son?" Her voice broke. "Because, he won't understand if you just disappear and don't come back."

Chase came to his feet. "Of course I'll say goodbye to Riley. I'll do anything I can to make it easier on him."

"Anything except stick around." She glared at him, wiping the back of her hand beneath her shimmering eyes.

It took everything Chase had not to pull her into his arms.

"I'll do what I can," he promised.

"Thanks for that." She headed for the door.

Chase opened his mouth to call after her. He didn't know why. There was nothing he could say. He was getting what he wanted. She was leaving now, and she knew it was for the best.

Chapter Ten

ONCE AGAIN, THE last place Maddy wanted to be was the stands at the AEBR bull rides. But Riley was beside her, and he was cheering on the riders, waiting patiently for his uncle Zane's turn. He was happy, at least for the moment. And she was letting him have the moment.

"Next up," called the announcer, "coming out of chute five, a veteran rider from Marietta, Montana who loves to show the young bucks how it's done. Ladies and gentlemen, give a great big Missoula welcome to Rory Douglas!"

The chute opened, and the black bull shot out, all four legs high in the air. Rory hung on mightily, but it was clear he was off balance right off the bat. Maddy held her breath while Riley shouted. "Ride 'im. Ride 'im."

But far too quickly Rory went airborne and came down in the cloud of dust. The crowd groaned in disappointment.

As the bullfighters attempted to corral the bull, Rory limped his way to the fence, and the crowd settled back into their seats. She saw Eli appear down front and he climbed the grandstand stairs to their fifth row seats.

"Hey," he said simply, taking the spot next to her on the

bench.

"Hi," she answered, grateful for the distraction of the recalcitrant bull.

The safety man rode past on horseback in front of them, whirling a lasso over his head, closing in on the bull.

Riley stood and mimicked the cowboy's motions.

Maddy loved all of her brothers. But under the circumstances, Eli was the one person who could make her evening even worse tonight. She was mortified that he'd caught her with Chase.

Eli leaned in close to her. "So, is Chase backing out of the deal then?"

Maddy turned and pulled back to better focus on Eli's face. She's expected a question about her sex life.

"The Douglas Ranch," Eli elaborated. "Did he tell you he was backing out?"

She almost laughed. Eli wasn't worried about her virtue. He was worried about the family economics. She didn't know whether to feel insulted or glad to be finally considered an adult.

"What's so funny?" Eli asked.

"Chase and I didn't talk about the Douglas Ranch."

The clouds billowing above the rolling hills chose that moment to rumble ominously.

Eli frowned. "Then what was so important that he had to kick me out?"

"What was important..." Maddy's throat grew thick

with repressed emotion. She didn't want to admit it, but there was no way to keep it a secret from her brothers. "Was to break things off with me."

Eli's expression darkened. "What?"

"You heard me." She had no desire to repeat herself.

She glanced at Riley to make sure his attention was still on the arena. It was. The bull had just been lassoed and was being led out of the arena.

"Why would he do that? Why would *anyone* do that?" The bewilderment in Eli's tone was a small balm to her ego.

She didn't want to tell him. But she didn't want to hold it inside either. She desperately needed comfort, and her hard-edged brother Eli was the only person around.

She whispered. "Chase doesn't believe that I love him."

It took Eli a moment to respond. "Do you?"

She tried to answer, but the words wouldn't come. Instead, she tipped her head onto Eli's shoulder.

Thunder rumbled again, lightening pale in the dark gray clouds.

Her brother swore softly under his breath. Then he put a strong arm around her and drew her close. "You want me to do something?" he asked gruffly. "I already decked him once, but I'll do it again. Harder."

She shook her head against him. "You can't help me with this. But thanks."

"...our next rider, Zane Merrick, coming out of chute one," came the announcer's voice.

Riley batted her arm. "Mommy, here he comes. Here comes Uncle Zane." He stretched up in his seat for a better view.

Just then, Maddy caught sight of Piper and Tristan heading along the stands toward them.

She swallowed hard and pulled her emotions together. She caught Piper's gaze and pointed to the arena to make sure they knew Zane was about to ride.

Piper smiled then her gaze rested on Eli for a moment, and the smile dimmed. She said something to Tristan who nodded and turned to go back. Then she held up one finger to Maddy, signaling she had something to do. She followed her son.

The maneuver puzzled Maddy. What could be so important that they'd miss Zane's ride?

The crowd's roar went up, and Maddy quickly turned her attention to Zane on the back of Over Easy.

Her brother came out of the chute looking good. The bull was aggressive, his back legs kicking high as he spun to the left. He shook his head back and forth, and his whole body shuddered, rattling Zane like a rag doll. But Zane hung on. Over Easy twisted his spine, reversing direction to spin right. Zane had a bad moment, but quickly got right.

The horn sounded, and Riley jumped to his feet, waving his little Stetson in the air. "Yippee! Good ride, Uncle Zane!" he called, beaming.

Then he settled back in his seat and looked to Maddy.

"Where's Daddy?"

"Chase isn't riding tonight," she said, keeping her voice light and her smile in place.

"He should be watchin'. He must be watchin'. Do you suppose he's behind the chutes?"

"He's probably behind the chutes," she agreed, grateful that Riley had supplied an answer to his own question.

"You okay?" Eli asked her in an undertone.

Maddy wasn't used to this kind of TLC from her second oldest brother. He'd be the first to step into a fight for her, but the last one she'd expect to worry about her emotions.

"I will be," she said.

"You want someone to talk to? I could go get Piper." There was a distinct note of discomfort in his voice as he made the offer.

Now that sounded more like the Eli she knew.

"She'll be back in a minute," Maddy said.

As they announced Zane's score of eighty-seven, Eli shifted in his seat beside her.

"You can take off," she told him. "I'll be fine."

"You sure?"

"I'm sure. Here she comes now." Piper was making her way along the walkway, moving slowly, a pensive expression on her face.

"I'm outta here," Eli said, coming to his feet. In seconds, he was down the staircase and off in the opposite direction.

Piper picked up her pace as the announcer chatted up the

next rider. The rain clattered on the overhead roof, blowing mist in from the open sides of the stands.

"Just in time," Piper said as she sat down.

She offered Riley a mini doughnut.

Riley happily dug one out of the sugared treats. "The bulls are gonna get wet," he sang.

"That's not all that's going to get wet," Piper said, glancing beside them. They were at the end of the row and the wind was blowing toward them.

She offered Maddy a doughnut, sympathy in her expression. "I know it's going to take a lot more than one."

Maddy accepted, trying for a smile. She'd told Piper what had happened, confessing the debacle in all its glory. Piper had staunchly blamed Chase for making love to her and then breaking it off. But it wasn't his fault, the lovemaking part anyway. Maddy had literally thrown herself in his arms.

"We can leave early if you want," Piper said. "If we take off tomorrow morning, you won't have to see him again."

"He said he'd say goodbye to Riley." Maddy wasn't sure what that would look like, and she dreaded it. But she was positive it would be better if Riley had a goodbye than if Chase simply disappeared from his life—like his real father had.

She felt tears threatening again.

"Don't let him do that to you," Piper said in an undertone. "He doesn't deserve it."

Piper was right. However wonderful Chase had seemed in the short term. He was never going to stick it out. Maddy should have seen it coming.

IT WAS AFTER midnight when Chase left the bull riders' after-party. He hadn't felt like socializing, but he sure hadn't felt like going back to his motel room either. So he'd had more than his fair share of whiskey shots trying to dull the pain. Luckily it was only a short walk back to the motel.

At the bottom of stairs of the honkytonk where he'd left the throbbing music and raucous crowds behind, Chase came face to face with a wall of Merrick brothers. They were shoulder to shoulder, feet planted apart, arms across their chests.

"Gotta talk to you," Lucas said.

Chase wasn't afraid. He doubted the Merricks would resort to physical violence. Even if they did, he'd bet money they weren't four on one fighters. At most, he'd have to duke it out with Eli. And Chase was kind of itching for a rematch. And he was just drunk enough not to give a crap about the pain.

"Sorry about the ranch," he said. "But I'm afraid the deal's not going to work out."

"You think we care about the land?" Lucas asked.

"We care about our sister," Eli said.

"What are you going to do about *that*?" Zane asked.

"You swore to me." Lucas's voice all but shook.

"You going to let the guy say anything at all?" Wyatt asked his brothers.

"There's no defense," Eli said.

"Still…" Wyatt added meaningfully.

"I know I'd like to hear his excuse," Zach said, pasting Chase with a narrow-eyed glare.

"I do like you, Wyatt," Chase said, appreciating the one brother's self-control.

"I don't particularly like you," Wyatt returned.

The conciliatory approach was obviously off the table.

"You're going to have a hard time believing this," Chase told them. "But I care about Maddy."

Eli gave a snort of derision.

"You want to hear what I have to say?" Chase asked him. "Or do you want to go straight to the fistfight?"

"We're not here to fight," Wyatt said.

"I'm not what she needs," Chase returned, suddenly feeling stone cold sober.

"You're what she wants," Lucas said.

"I'm what she *thinks* she wants. You must see it."

"I don't see anything," Zane said.

"I'm the replacement for everything she lost," Chase enunciated, making sure there could be no misunderstanding. "I'm the shadow of Chase Barrett. Right now she thinks that's all she deserves. But it's *not* all she deserves. And one day she's going to figure that out. And when she does, she won't leave me."

Now that he'd started, Chase couldn't stop. "She *won't* leave me, because she'll be so invested in our little family, and she won't want to hurt Riley, and she'll know, she'll know by then without a shadow of doubt that I'm completely in love with her. And she won't want to hurt me either, because she never wants to hurt anyone. So, she'll stick it out. She'll be unhappy. But she'll stick it out to all the way to that day when she can't stand it anymore, and then she'll leave me. And she'll feel like a failure, even though she's not. She's the most amazing woman on this earth. And she deserves better than the future I see rolling out in front of us. I'm not going to do that to her. And you shouldn't ask me to do that to her."

Chase stopped. He snapped his jaw shut. He'd said way more than he'd intended, but once the ball had started rolling, it had gotten completely away from him. He obviously wasn't as sober as he felt.

All four brothers were now staring at him in stunned silence.

"That wasn't what I was expecting," Lucas finally said.

"I feel like I want to thank him," Zane said.

"Why did you let it get this far?" Eli asked.

Chase saw no point in holding back now. "Because I thought I had a shot. By the time I accepted reality, everything had gotten way out of control. Walking away is now my only option."

"What about yesterday?" Eli challenged, his tone edgy.

His brothers all looked to him with curiosity. It was obvious he hadn't told them about finding Maddy in Chase's hotel room.

"Yesterday, I slipped," Chase admitted. "It was a mistake. But, she—" He stopped himself again. "This is definitely too much information."

"I feel like I want him on the team," Wyatt said.

"You think there's any chance…" Lucas ventured.

"Chase Barrett wasn't that great a husband," Zane put in. "He cheated on her."

The revelation surprised Chase.

"Maybe if you told her that," Eli said.

"You want me to denounce her dead husband in order to make her love me?" Even if he thought it would work, Chase couldn't see doing that.

"I suppose," Wyatt said, obviously taking Chase's point.

"I'm not sure you should give up so easily," Lucas said.

"Have you not been *listening*?" Chase's voice rose. "She's convinced herself that she loves me. She'll commit to anything right now. It's only later, after she realizes it was a mistake…" He wasn't going to go through the logical all over again.

"He's right," Wyatt said.

"So we just give up?" Zane asked.

"Just so we're clear," Chase said, feeling dark amusement

creeping in. "I'm breaking it off with your sister, not with you all."

"We feel jilted all the same," Lucas said.

"I am sorry about the ranch," Chase said. "I think I would have liked being in business with you."

"We would have liked it too," Wyatt said.

AT THE WILDWOOD Café down the street from the motel, Riley dug into his pancakes while Maddy toyed with the omelet on her plate. Her son was an early riser, and she couldn't help but think he might make a good rancher someday. Piper and Tristan's room had been dark and quiet when Maddy left an hour ago. She hadn't even glanced at Chase's room. The less she let herself think about him, the better.

Wyatt startled her, appearing suddenly at the table. "Morning, little sister."

Maddy felt a small lift in her mood. "Hi, Wyatt. I didn't know you were still here."

He pulled out a chair and sat down. "Hi there, Riley."

"Hi, Uncle Wyatt. I'm having strawberry syrup."

"That's my favorite," Wyatt said.

"It's pink. Does it make my tongue pink?" Riley stuck out his tongue.

"Not while you're eating, Riley," Maddy warned.

"Sorry, Mommy."

"He's great," Wyatt said to her.

"He is," Maddy agreed.

"I heard what happened."

Maddy mentally braced herself. "You talked to Eli?"

"And to Lucas and to Zane, and to Chase for that matter."

Her stomach contracted at the sound of Chase's name.

Wyatt flipped over the white stoneware coffee cup in front of him. "How much do you know about our plans for the Douglas Ranch?"

"Not much. Eli said something about Chase planning to buy it with you. But he seemed to think Chase would walk because Eli hit him." She thought about stopping there. But she wouldn't let herself take the coward's way out. "Then again, me sleeping with Chase was probably the real problem."

"It does complicate things," Wyatt said with a wry smile.

"I'm glad you think this is funny." Her eyes were starting to tingle.

His expression neutralized. "I don't think it's funny, Maddy. I'm really sorry you got hurt. But you're a grown woman, and you made a choice, you took a chance. Sometimes these things work out, and sometimes they don't."

"How very philosophical of you." Maddy would have appreciated a little more compassion. She took a sip of her coffee, struggling to stay tough in front of Wyatt.

The waitress came by, filled their coffee cups, and took his order for a five-star breakfast.

"What were the mathematical odds, Button?" he asked as the young woman walked away.

"The mathematical odds of what?"

"That Chase Garrett would wander into your life, be mistaken by Riley…" Wyatt glanced at his nephew and let the sentence hang. "Fall in love with you. You fall in love with him. And your family be magically put back together."

She got his point. She didn't like it, but she understood how he would think that. "I didn't exactly do the math."

"I believe the technical term is astronomical."

"So what?"

"So, you can understand Chase's skepticism."

Maddy could feel the conversation taking a turn. Her guard went up. "What do you know about Chase's skepticism?"

"He thinks you don't really love him."

"Well, he's wrong."

Wyatt gave a nod and took a sip of his coffee. "Let's say he is."

"He *is*."

"I just accepted your premise, Maddy."

She sat back in her chair, compressing her lips. Wyatt was supposed to be the smart, thoughtful brother. She couldn't figure out why he was being so difficult.

"You love him," Wyatt stated.

She did.

"So what do you want?"

That was a ridiculous question.

"*Him*," she said.

"And what are you doing?"

Her growing frustration turned into sarcasm. "I'm eating breakfast."

Wyatt looked at the omelet, hash browns, and fruit on her plate. "You're not, but that's not what I meant. What are you going to do about Chase?"

"I tried, Wyatt." She lowered her voice. "I put it out there, and he threw it back in my face."

"He doesn't want to hurt you, and he doesn't want to hurt Riley."

"Well, that's exactly what he's doing."

"I'm not hurt," Riley said. "I'm rough and tough and hard to bluff."

Despite everything, Maddy couldn't stop a smile.

"Courtesy of Zane?" Wyatt asked.

"From Zane," she confirmed. Riley was overly fond of quoting his uncle.

"You are tough," Wyatt told Riley.

Riley had lost interest in his pancakes and was drawing on his place mat with the crayons provided by the restaurant.

"This is the white bull," he said. "It has five spots."

"That's a good drawing," Maddy told him, admiring his effort.

"You're giving up?" Wyatt asked her.

"I didn't go down easily," she defended herself.

Wyatt's expression turned thoughtful. "He seems like a really good guy."

"He is a really good guy. He's a great guy. He's the guy I should have been with all along."

Now Wyatt was watching her intently. "Tell me what that means."

"It means I'm not replacing what I lost. It means I can tell the difference." She felt a sense of righteousness well up inside her.

"The difference?"

"Yes. I know I love Chase Garrett, because I never loved..." She chose her words carefully in case Riley was listening. "*Before.*"

Wyatt broke into a smile.

"What?" She didn't understand how that was amusing.

"Tell him *that*," Wyatt said with conviction. "All of that. You know what you want, little sister. You know what you know. Take the bull by the horns and wrestle him to the ground already."

"The bull by the horns?" She almost smiled at that.

"It seemed like an apt metaphor." Wyatt gave a mock toast with his coffee cup. "Don't let Chase make up your mind for you. Fight for what you want."

"Now you sound like Eli."

"I obviously don't mean with your fists. Use your head,

Button. You've always been smarter than the rest of us."

"You're the smart one," she said. "I'm the pretty one."

"You're the compassionate one. But don't be nice to Chase this time."

She let Wyatt's words sink in. And they did sink in.

The waitress arrived with his breakfast, and Maddy took a first bite of her omelet.

She didn't know what she was going to do, and she sure didn't know how she was going to do it. But she *was* going to fight for Chase, even if that meant fighting against him.

CHASE HAD NO intention of sticking around for the finals tonight. He'd finish his breakfast, track Riley down for a quick goodbye then get on the road for Tacoma. He'd ride next weekend come hell or high water.

He'd rehearsed an explanation to Riley. He'd tell him he was going bull riding and that he'd likely be gone for a long time. It wasn't the perfect solution, but it was the best Chase could come up with right now. Any move he made beyond a speedy exit would only make things worse.

A shadow appeared across the outdoor patio table. He gave an inward sigh and raised his gaze, not ready to talk to anyone at all.

"Hi, Chase."

"Patrick?" Chase was dumbfounded by the sight of his

former friend.

"Can I talk to you?" There was hesitancy, even fear in Patrick's voice.

He was smart to be afraid. He should have stayed far, far away from Chase, and he should have done that forever.

"No, you can't talk to me," Chase answered sharply, rising from his chair. He pulled out his wallet and tossed a couple of bills on the table.

"*Chase,*" Patrick pleaded.

"You lost the right to talk to me seven months ago." Chase's tone stayed hard as he strode for the sidewalk.

Patrick followed. "I'm only asking for a minute."

"I don't have a minute."

"Seriously? I've come all the way from Twin River Valley, and you don't have a minute to listen?"

Chase kept walking. "There is nothing you can say that I want to hear."

"I came to say I'm sorry."

Chase almost laughed out loud. Patrick thought an apology was going to make a difference?

"Chase, man, I'm going crazy here."

"You're going crazy? You stole me fiancée, my future, and *you're* going crazy." Chase increased his pace, heading along the sidewalk through the crowds of shoppers and tourists.

"That's the thing," Patrick said.

The traffic light in front of him turned red and Chase

took an abrupt left turn, crossing the opposite street. He had no idea where he was going, and he didn't care.

Patrick kept pace. "I wake up every morning, sick to my stomach, feeling guilty as hell for what I did."

"Good."

"I come home to my wife and my daughter, and all I can feel is terrible."

"And you want absolution from me?"

Patrick felt terrible? How did he think Chase felt about it all?

And then the words hit him. A daughter?

"All these months, and I still can't get past what I did," Patrick continued.

At the mental image of a baby girl, something unexpectedly shifted inside Chase. Under any other circumstances, he'd be thrilled for Patrick. He'd be asking for pictures and smoking a cigar. He found his pace slowing down.

"I'm not looking for your forgiveness," Patrick said, his tone going quieter.

Chase wanted to ask about the baby. He wanted to ask about Laura-Leigh.

"Every day," Patrick said. "All I can think is that it should have been you. I stole your life, Chase. I had no right to steal your life."

They were across the street now, in front of an ice cream parlor playing chirpy music.

Chase stopped and the crowds parted around them.

"The price was too high." Patrick's voice went hollow. "You paid it, and I had no right to make you do that."

"It's not my life," Chase found himself saying.

Patrick seemed surprised that Chase had spoken. Then he looked puzzled.

"It's not my life," Chase repeated. It was suddenly crystal clear, and he wondered why it had taken him so long to figure it out.

Patrick wasn't living Chase's life. Patrick was living his own life that had happened at one point to include betraying his best friend. But Laura-Leigh had loved Patrick. It wasn't her fault she loved him. It wasn't Patrick's fault he'd loved her back. And it sure wasn't any fault of their innocent newborn baby girl.

Patrick was gaping at him in obvious confusion.

"You shouldn't feel guilty," Chase said, looking directly into Patrick's eyes for the first time.

"Why?"

Patrick wasn't living Chase's life. The words boomed inside Chase's brain.

An enormous weight seemed to lift from his shoulders. If Patrick wasn't living Chase's life, then maybe, just *maybe*, Chase wasn't living Chase Barrett's life either.

"What's her name?" Chase asked Patrick.

"Who?" Patrick's puzzlement seemed to be increasing.

"Your daughter. What's your daughter's name?"

"Elizabeth."

"That's nice," Chase said with a smile.

"Uh, Chase?"

Chase clapped his friend on the shoulder. "You don't need to feel guilty. I know you didn't fall in love with Laura-Leigh to hurt me."

"You know, I'd have given anything…" The emotional strain cracked Patrick's voice.

"I know." Chase now knew that was true.

Neither Patrick nor Laura-Leigh had set out to hurt him. He remembered their expressions on that terrible night. He'd been blinded by anger, but they'd both been devastated by how it had all played out.

He'd never truly loved Laura-Leigh. Not the way he loved Maddy. He loved Maddy beyond reason, eclipsing any feelings he'd ever had for anyone else.

And there was a chance Maddy felt the same about him. There was a chance she recognized it better than he did. If there was even the slightest chance, Chase was taking it.

He was suddenly impatient. He had to get going. Patrick was going to have to wait.

"Are they here?" he asked Patrick. "Laura-Leigh and Elizabeth? Did they come with you?"

"No."

He took a half-step back towards the fairgrounds. "I'd love to see Laura-Leigh sometime and to meet Elizabeth. And you and I should sit down, have a drink. But not right now. Later? Tonight? Can you stay?"

Patrick broke into a smile. "Yes. I can stay."

"There's something I have to do."

"Chase, I never…"

"I'm happy for you," Chase said. "It was ugly, but it turned out right."

"Thank you." Patrick's voice was thick as he stuck out his hand to shake.

Chase took it. Then he pulled Patrick into a hug. "It's going to be fine. It's going to be good."

"Yeah?" Patrick gave a tight nod as the two men separated.

"Later," said Chase as he moved away.

Right now he had to find Maddy. He'd done something incredibly stupid, and he was going to undo it or die trying.

Chapter Eleven

CHASE HAD PROMISED he'd say goodbye to Riley, and Maddy knew he'd never go back on his word. So Piper had hidden Riley away where Chase wouldn't be able to find him.

Maybe Maddy was a bad mother for using her son that way. But it was the only advantage she had, the only surefire way of trying one more time to make Chase see reason before he disappeared from her life altogether.

She made her way across the fairgrounds past the bull enclosures, straining to see through the growing crowd on finals day. Chase hadn't been in his motel room. That was the first place she'd checked. He wasn't at any of the three closest cafés. And she'd done a complete lap of the fairgrounds without finding him.

She turned around now and was making her way in the opposite direction. The beer gardens were in front of her, but they were closed this early in the day. There was only a smattering of people at the pens, and the stands were empty. Most of the crowds were at the concession stands and exhibitors tents.

It was getting hot, and she was growing disheartened, wondering if she'd already missed her chance.

But then she spotted him, far away in the distance.

He was walking away from her, heading for the parking lot. It looked like he was leaving. Maybe, despite her best efforts, he'd already found Riley, said his goodbyes, and was about to drive away.

She broke into a run, past the food trucks and the barns, along the road that led to the parking lot. Her baby toe started to sting, and she cursed the cowboy boots that were also chafing her bare calves. They definitely weren't made for running.

The sun grew hotter, and she started to sweat in her T-shirt.

"Chase!" she finally called as she grew closer.

He didn't turn.

"Chase!" she called louder this time.

He turned, spotting her. "Maddy?" His expression turned to concern. "What's wrong? Is it Riley?"

She shook her head, gasping for breath. "I... I..."

"You're scaring me."

"Nothing's wrong," she managed.

Well, a lot was wrong. But nothing new was wrong.

"Good." He rested his hands on her shoulders. "We need to talk."

"No," she told him sharply, shaking him off. She wasn't going through that again.

He'd had a chance to say his piece, and now it was her turn.

"Don't talk," she ordered him. "Just listen."

"But—"

"It's my turn now." Her breathing was coming back under control. She searched her brain for a starting point, knowing how much was at stake. "You've met Wyatt, right? Well, he's my smart brother. He's cool, calm, and collected under just about any circumstance. It comes with being a pilot, I guess. But I just talked to him."

Chase looked puzzled, but thankfully stayed quiet.

Maddy was procrastinating, but she was afraid to take the plunge. This was her last chance, and she didn't want to blow this. She forced herself to push ahead. "I told him I was in love with you."

Chase opened his mouth.

She clapped her hand over it. "No. Still my turn."

He heaved a sigh, but gave a nod.

"Thing is." She relaxed. The urgency drained out of her. Her hand relaxed on his mouth. "Thing is, Chase. I never loved my husband."

Chase's eyes widened.

"I was pregnant, and he took responsibility. He married me, and we tried really hard to make it work. For Riley. We both loved Riley. But he was away a lot. And there were women. I know there were women. And I guess I can understand it. I mean, our sex life was never that great. And we didn't have all that much to talk about. I got frustrated, and he stayed away even more."

For a split-second, she thought back to those lonely days, when she wondered if that would be her fate for her entire life. "And then he was killed. I was sad, of course. I liked him. But it was strange. People thought I was something I wasn't. They thought I was a devastated, heartbroken, grieving widow. It was more like losing a friend. And it was so sad for Riley. Don't get me wrong, Riley worshipped his daddy, and he missed him terribly. And I wouldn't wish that on any child."

"Can I talk yet?" Chase asked against her hand.

"No. You can't. You talked last time, and it all went bad. I love you. I love *you*, Chase Garrett. I'm not mixing you up with anybody else. It has nothing to do with Riley. Though I love, love, love that you love Riley."

Chase's eyes crinkled with laughter. "There's something wrong with that sentence."

"Shut up."

"Yes, ma'am."

"I know you don't trust my feelings. But *I* trust my feelings. And Wyatt trusts my feelings. Did I tell you Wyatt is my smart brother?"

Chase nodded.

"Well, he is. And he's right. And more importantly, I'm right. I'm not your ex fiancée. I'm not ever going to wish you were another man. I'm not going to leave you. I'm *never* going to leave you Chase Garrett." She paused for a breath. "That is, if I can convince you to stay with me in the first place."

"Please tell me it's my turn now."

She searched her brain, trying to figure out if she'd remembered to say everything. "Also, you're a great lover."

Chase grasped her wrist and pulled her hand from his mouth. Then he swooped in and captured her lips in a long, deep, passionate kiss. Before it ended, his arms were wrapped tightly around her waist, and she was clinging to him, and every nerve in her body was singing with happiness.

He finally pulled away and she felt like she floated back to earth.

She found her voice. "I don't know what that means."

"That's because you wouldn't keep quiet long enough to let me say anything."

"I had a lot to say, and I didn't want you to mess up my rhythm."

His eyes were light with joy. "The last thing I want to do, Maddy, is mess up your rhythm."

Her heart felt lighter. This didn't look like a man who was about to walk away from her.

"What did you want to say?" she asked.

"I can't remember."

She socked him in the arm with the end of her fist.

He laughed. "I love you, Maddy."

"I know." She sobered, her nervousness returning. "Yesterday, that wasn't enough."

"It's always been enough for me," he said, drawing her in close. "I was worried about you. I couldn't believe I could be lucky enough to have you love me back."

"Then you should count yourself lucky."

"I do."

"You believe me?"

"I do. Now tell me again that I'm a great lover."

"I'd rather show you."

He glanced around them. "Now?"

"Well, back at the motel."

"Where's Riley?"

"He's with Piper. She's hiding him."

"What? Why?"

"So you couldn't say goodbye to him and leave town. I was determined to find you, Chase. I was determined to change your mind."

He smiled and smoothed back her windblown hair. "I've been looking for you. All those things you just said to me? I was about to say them to you." He paused. "Well, not all of them. There were quite a lot." His tone softened. "I wanted to say I believed you, Maddy. I realized this morning that I wasn't your husband's shadow. Riley may have been confused, but you were never confused."

"I wasn't confused for a second," she said.

Chase Garrett was his own man. He was unique. He was second to none. And he was everything she'd ever wanted.

"Marry me," Chase said.

"I will."

He kissed her again. It was long and sweet and satisfying, promising years of wonderful things to come.

"We need to find your brothers."

She walked her fingertips up his chest. "I don't think we need my brothers for what we're about to do."

"You're right," Chase said. "The Douglas Ranch can wait. I can't." He took her hand.

CHASE TUCKED RILEY into his own bed back in Deadwood. Riley's eyes fluttered closed, and he was asleep in seconds. He'd blown out the four candles on his cake, opened all his presents, and completely charmed his uncles who'd all come to town for the occasion.

Chase could hear the conversation down the hall. Patrick and Laura-Leigh were there, with three-month-old Elizabeth. She was a beautiful baby, never more so than when she was in Maddy's arms, making Chase think about the future, about having a baby with Maddy and how perfect it would be to give Riley some brothers and sisters.

"Is he out?" came Maddy's soft voice in the doorway behind him.

"Like a light," Chase said, rising.

"He's going to get spoiled by all those uncles."

"I wouldn't worry. There'll be plenty of work for him to do on the ranch in Montana." Chase gave Riley's soft hair a final stroke as he moved from the bed. "Nothing like hard work to build character."

After the cake was cleared away, the paperwork for the Douglas Ranch purchase had been spread out on the kitchen table. They were finalizing details tonight, and the "For Sale" sign was already up in Maddy's front yard.

Chase took her hand as they made their way back down the hall.

"We'll need the deposit next week," Lucas said when he spotted Chase.

"No problem," Chase replied. "I'm very liquid."

After selling in Lethbridge, he'd kept his investments in redeemable bonds. With one phone call, he'd have all the cash they needed.

"I like liquidity in a future brother-in-law," Lucas said.

"I like a man who knows cattle," Eli said.

Chase had decided to leave the AEBR circuit. He had absolutely no desire to be on the road and away from Maddy and Riley. So he and Eli would run the Douglas Ranch, to be renamed Merrick-Garrett.

"I should head home," Piper said, rising from her chair.

Lucas watched her from across the room, his mouth tightening at the corners.

Chase had noticed that Lucas and Piper had continued to avoid each other.

Now Chase saw that Eli was watching Piper too. He didn't look angry. In fact, for a split second there seemed to be a yearning in his expression. But it was gone before Chase could be sure.

Chase tipped his head close to Maddy. "What's with Piper and Eli?"

She looked puzzled. "Nothing. Why?"

"No reason." He could easily have been mistaken.

"Her problem is with Lucas."

"I know. They're trying to hide it tonight, but it's pretty obvious. Where's Tristan?"

"Out with his friends. Piper wasn't thrilled about that, but she didn't want him moping around here and putting a damper on the party."

"I remember being fifteen." Chase had to say he was sympathetic.

What teenager wants to attend a four-year-old's birthday party with a bunch of his mother's friends?

"I'm outta here too," said Zane. "Can you give me a lift into town?" he asked Piper.

"Sure."

With Zane, Chase noted, she seemed perfectly relaxed.

"Good luck in Sacramento." Maddy gave her twin brother a hug.

The party broke up, with Lucas heading back to New York on a red-eye and Wyatt flying off first thing in the morning. Chase and Eli would finalize the contracts and do a site inspection of the Douglas Ranch.

As the last brother headed out the door, Maddy turned into Chase's arms.

He gave her a kiss on the temple. "Tired?" he asked.

"Not too tired," she said with a smile in her voice.

"So, we can celebrate Riley's birthday?" Chase teased, loving the anticipation of taking her to bed.

She held up her left hand, fingers spread, admiring the new, winking solitaire. "That and this gorgeous ring you just gave me."

He kissed her finger. "I'm sorry it took a few days. I wanted it to be perfect."

"It is perfect. You're perfect."

"So are you." His heart swelled with love and contentment as they walked down the hallway, her head on his shoulder. "That's what makes us perfect together."

The End

The American Extreme Bull Riders Tour

If you enjoyed *Chase*, you'll love the rest of the American Extreme Bull Riders Tour!

Book 1: *Tanner* by Sarah Mayberry

Book 2: *Chase* by Barbara Dunlop

Book 3: *Casey* by Kelly Hunter

Book 4: *Cody* by Megan Crane

Book 5: *Troy* by Amy Andrews

Book 6: *Kane* by Sinclair Jayne

Book 7: *Austin* by Jeannie Watt

Book 8: *Gage* by Katherine Garbera

Available now at your favorite online retailer!

If you enjoyed *Chase*, don't miss Barbara Dunlop's new series...

The Match Series

The comedic, contemporary romance series featuring the high-tech antics of matchmaking senior citizens unleashed on their unsuspecting heirs

Book 1: *An Unlikely Match*

Book 2: *An Impractical Match*

Book 3: *An Extraordinary Match*

Book 4: *An Astonishing Match*

Book 5: *An Unpredictable Match*

Available now at your favorite online retailer!

About the Author

Barbara Dunlop is a New York Times and USA Today bestselling author of fifty romance novels. A three time finalist in the prestigious RITA award, she is also a two time winner of the RWA Golden Heart award. An Unlikely Match, the first book in her acclaimed Match series, was a number one bestseller on Amazon. Barbara makes her home in Yukon with her bush pilot husband and the moose and bears that wander through their yard.

Visit Barbara at BarbaraDunlop.com

Thank you for reading

Chase

If you enjoyed this book, you can find more from all our great authors at TulePublishing.com, or from your favorite online retailer.

TULE
PUBLISHING

96894633R00154

Made in the USA
Lexington, KY
24 August 2018